ARENA OF DANGER

Suddenly a shadow appeared over the upper edge of the stadium. Joe squinted into the sun and saw the outline of a helicopter coming in for a landing.

Frank stopped applauding when he saw the unmarked black craft descend into the center of the arena. A quick glance at Rosa's shocked expression told him this was not part of the show.

In the ring Rigo was shielding his eyes from the dust kicked up by the chopper's downdraft, so he didn't see a man dressed in army camouflage fatigues, wearing a black ski mask, and carrying an automatic rifle emerge from the chopper's side door. The man sprinted a short distance across the ring and grabbed Rigo by his collar.

Joe watched as the gunman dragged Rigo to the helicopter and threw him inside. The chopper began to rise and turn, kicking up a swirl of reddish dust before it cleared the edge of the stadium and headed out over the city.

Books in THE HARDY BOYS CASEFILES™ Series

Available from ARCHWAY Paperbacks

THE HARDY BOYS

CASEFILES™

NO. 109

MOMENT OF TRUTH

FRANKLIN W. DIXON

AN ARCHWAY PAPERBACK
Published by POCKET BOOKS
New York London Toronto Sydney Tokyo Singapore

This book is a work of fiction. Names, characters, places and incidents are products of the author's imagination or are used fictitiously. Any resemblance to actual events or locales or persons, living or dead, is entirely coincidental.

AN ARCHWAY PAPERBACK *Original*

An Archway Paperback published by
POCKET BOOKS, a division of Simon & Schuster Inc.
1230 Avenue of the Americas, New York, NY 10020

Copyright © 1996 by Simon & Schuster Inc.
Produced by Mega-Books, Inc.

ISBN: 0-671-50432-0

First Archway Paperback printing March 1996

10 9 8 7 6 5 4 3 2 1

THE HARDY BOYS, AN ARCHWAY PAPERBACK and colophon are registered trademarks of Simon & Schuster Inc.

THE HARDY BOYS CASEFILES is a trademark of Simon & Schuster Inc.

Cover photograph from "The Hardy Boys" series © 1995 Nelvana Limited/Marathon Productions S.A. All Rights Reserved.

Logo Design™ & © 1995 by Nelvana Limited. All Rights Reserved.

Printed in the U.S.A.

IL 6+

MOMENT OF TRUTH

Chapter

1

FRANK HARDY SAW her first. He and his brother, Joe, were paddling their surfboards out toward the breakers about a hundred yards off South Padre Island, Texas. Frank noticed the girl riding the curl of a good-size wave with an agility that made him envious. With her raven black hair streaming behind her, she looked to Frank like a mermaid balancing on the back of a playful porpoise. She was tall and slender, and her skin was the color of brown sugar.

"Isn't that the girl who was working behind the counter at the surf shop?" Joe asked Frank as they paused to rest. The beach behind them was crawling with high school and college students enjoying spring break under the warm Texas sun on the Gulf of Mexico.

"That's not a girl, Joe," Frank said. "That's a goddess."

Joe could see what his brother meant as he watched the girl finish riding the wave and kick out gracefully not ten yards from them. When she crouched down to straddle her board and sank waist-deep into the salty foam, Joe shouted, "Is that a magic carpet under you?"

She flashed a smile at the two brothers. "No, I don't believe in magic," she shouted back in slightly accented English.

Sculling their boards toward the young woman, Frank and Joe introduced themselves. "We're Frank and Joe Hardy from Bayport," Frank said, brushing back his wet, brown hair. "That's up north, where it's still snowing."

"I'm Rosa Galvan from Matamoros," she said, nodding toward the southern end of the huge beach in the direction of Mexico. "It's just across the border, a few miles south of here."

"Didn't I see you at the surf rental shop?" Joe asked.

"Yes," Rosa said, smiling. "I just got off work, so I thought I'd catch a few waves before I went home."

"Mind if we join you?" Frank asked. When she said yes, Frank shook his head. He couldn't believe their luck—the sun, the surf, and now a beautiful girl—all on their first day of spring break. When he caught the gleam

2

in his brother's eye, he could tell Joe felt the same way.

The three teenagers passed the afternoon skimming the waves, and by the time the sun was low in the sky, they were friends. "Do you want to meet after work again tomorrow?" Joe asked as they brushed the sand off their boards and stacked them against the rental shack.

Rosa shook her head. "Tomorrow's a special day. It's my brother's *alternativa.* Tomorrow my brother enters the bullfighting ring to become a matador," she announced proudly.

"Your brother's a bullfighter?" Joe asked, playfully holding out his towel as if it were a bullfighter's cape. *"Toro, toro,"* he muttered, narrowing his eyes, inviting Frank to charge. Frank chuckled and tried to strip the towel from Joe's hands.

"Have either of you ever seen a real bullfight?" Rosa asked.

"No, we haven't," Joe said.

"But of course we've heard about them," Frank said.

"I've heard it's pretty brutal," Joe said. "If the matador doesn't make a clean kill of the bull, then everybody figures he had a bad day at the office."

"I'm not sure I could be a regular fan of a sport where the object is to kill the animal," Frank said. "But I guess I'd like to see it once."

"I realize it's strong stuff," Rosa said. "Not many Americans have a taste for it, but it's an important ritual in my country."

"So let's check it out," Joe said. "Do we get to meet your brother?"

"Of course," Rosa said, gathering up her towel and beach bag and slipping on her sandals. "Rigo would be honored to meet you. I'll pick you up at ten."

"We're staying at the Casa del Mar apartments," Joe said. "Do you know where they are?"

"I do," Rosa said, putting on her sunglasses and walking toward her car. She looked back, a smile on her face. "My uncle Ramon owns them."

The next day Rosa picked up Frank and Joe and drove them across the Rio Grande into Matamoros. There was only a short wait at the border crossing, where the guards, who recognized Rosa, briefly checked the Hardys' passports. She parked her cherry red Jeep at an apartment house near the bullfighting ring. "Do you live here?" Frank asked.

"No," she replied. "My uncle's bodyguard lives here, but he said I could use his parking space."

"Your uncle has a bodyguard?" Joe inquired. "Why? Is he some kind of celebrity?"

"Oh, no," Rosa replied with a frown. "He

would hate that. He's in private business. He owns a lot of property on both sides of the border. He is a rancher, too, and he raises fighting bulls."

Frank gave a low whistle. "I'm impressed. From bulls to bodyguards. Sounds like somebody I'd like to meet."

"You will," Rosa replied. As they made their way along the crowded sidewalks toward the *plaza de toros,* Rosa told the Hardys that her older brother, Rigo, now nineteen, had been a novice bullfighter since he was sixteen. "Today is a special *fiesta brava,*" she said, "the first time for him to step into the ring as a real matador."

Plastered on the walls of the bullring were large, colorful posters of the bullfighters they would be seeing inside. "Who's El Puma?" Joe asked Rosa, slowly sounding out the Spanish words.

"That's Rigo," Rosa said. "In Spanish, *El Puma* means 'the panther.' They say that in the ring my brother is as brave and as beautiful as a panther."

Rosa led them down a narrow flight of stairs to the dressing rooms under the bullring. In the dark basement corridor, several doors lined the walls. They heard the shuffle of thousands of feet and the buzz of many voices above their heads as the stadium filled.

Outside Rigo's dressing room, a distinguished-looking middle-aged man in a blue suit, white shirt, and yellow silk tie was talking to three men wearing bullfighters' costumes with tight pants, short jackets, stockings, and slippers.

"Uncle Ramon," Rosa said, kissing her uncle on both cheeks. Ramon Galvan smiled and embraced his niece. Joe guessed he was about fifty, with jet black hair, a strong, straight nose, and deep-set brown eyes.

Rosa introduced Joe and Frank, and Galvan shook their hands. He introduced them to the three bullfighters. "These are Rigo's picadors," he explained. "They ride horses in the ring and are very important to the matador's safety."

Señor Galvan tapped on the dressing-room door and opened it. He ushered the Hardys and Rosa inside, then turned to greet some other well-wishers. In the small, candlelit room, they saw a handsome, well-built young man wearing dark green velvet knee-length pants trimmed in gold and soft black slippers.

Rosa introduced Joe and Frank to her brother Rigoberto, Rigo for short. With a shy smile, the young bullfighter held out his hand. "I am pleased to meet you," he said quietly.

"This is a real treat for us," Joe said. "It's the first time we've ever been to a bullfight, and we get to meet the matador."

"Your first bullfight?" Rigo said. "I hope you will not be disappointed."

"You seem awfully calm," Frank said, "considering you're about to go up against a three-thousand-pound animal in front of fifty thousand people."

"It's all part of the training," Rigo said. "If you know what you're doing, it's easy to avoid getting hurt. We learn to focus and shut out all distractions. I had a good teacher."

One of Rigo's assistants held out a short jacket, also dark green trimmed in gold. Rigo slipped it on over his white shirt and narrow black tie.

Sensing it was time to leave Rigo alone to finish his preparations, Frank said, "Thanks for taking the time to say hello, and good luck out there." Both brothers gave Rigo a strong handshake, and Joe flashed him a thumbs-up. Rigo smiled and flashed a thumbs-up back at Joe.

"A matador's suit is called a *traje de luces,*" Rosa said, walking Joe and Frank toward the door. "It means 'suit of lights.' Pale pink is the traditional color for the stockings," she added, turning to watch Rigo attach what looked like a round, black object to his hair at the nape of his neck. It became a short ponytail.

"Every matador wears a *coleta,*" Rosa said. "Rigo's is woven from strands of our dear mother's hair. She died five years ago."

7

"I'm sorry," Frank said. "If you don't mind talking about it, how did it happen?"

"Both my parents were schoolteachers in a village in southern Mexico," Rosa answered. "They were killed by government soldiers who thought they were revolutionaries." In the soft candlelight, Joe noticed her eyes tearing. "My uncle takes care of us now," Rosa continued. "He has raised Rigo and me as my parents would have wished."

An assistant handed Rigo a small black hat and a red cape, which he draped over his left shoulder. When he was fully dressed, Rigo stepped over to a small altar in a corner of the room and lit three candles. He knelt and prayed. "The candles will stay lit," Rosa whispered to Joe and Frank, "until Rigo returns. Come on, let us go to our seats."

The band was striking up what Rosa called a *paso doble*, a march, as the Hardys and Rosa settled into her uncle's ringside box. Rosa's uncle, Joe reflected, was obviously a man of privilege.

The matadors marched proudly into the ring of red sand. Joe could feel the electricity in the air. The crowd noise settled down to a low murmur. Suddenly a trumpet sounded and a large wooden door at one end of the arena opened with a bang. A huge black bull came racing out of the shadows and into the sunlight. The crowd roared its approval; the beast seemed to become enraged by the sound. It charged blindly toward the wall beneath Galvan's ringside seats. Frank instinctively jumped back when it slammed into the thick wood with a jolt that rattled the stands.

Ramon Galvan laughed and slapped Frank on the shoulder. "Don't worry, he can't get up here. But down there, he'd kill you."

Frank believed it. When Rigo appeared alone in the ring, looking small in his slippers and skintight uniform, Frank felt a wave of concern. In an instant, the bull turned, caught sight of Rigo, and charged.

Rigo held out his cape, shaking it tantalizingly until the bull reached him and raked its dagger-sharp horns across the red cloth, probing for the young man behind it. The huge animal passed impossibly close to Rigo's body. Rosa gasped and clutched Frank's hand, squeezing it.

Again and again the bull charged, and just as often Rigo danced gracefully out of reach. Each time the animal charged, Rigo made yet another graceful pass of the cape, barely avoiding the bull's swerving attacks. Each time, the crowd roared, "Olé!"

The bull's charges eventually became more sluggish and its haunches became drenched in sweat. Although Frank was sure Rigo was also tiring, he never showed it, maintaining his quickness and precision with each pass.

Almost before Frank realized what had happened, he saw Rigo's sword flash in the sun and then plunge cleanly into the bull's heart. Within seconds, it was over. The bull toppled and lay at Rigo's feet. As the crowd cheered, Rigo leaned down and kissed the huge animal on the forehead as a tribute to its courage. Then he stood, removed his hat, and bowed low to his fans.

"Viva El Puma!" the crowd shouted over and over. Hats and flowers rained down into the ring. Rosa hugged Joe, Frank, and her uncle. Tears of happiness glistened on her cheeks.

Then suddenly a shadow appeared over the upper edge of the stadium. Joe squinted into the sun and saw the outline of a helicopter coming in for a landing. Over the roar of the crowd he could hear the *ack-ack* of the chopper's blades.

Frank stopped applauding when he saw the unmarked black craft descend into the center of the arena. A quick glance at Rosa's shocked expression told him this was not part of the show.

In the ring Rigo was shielding his eyes from the dust kicked up by the chopper's downdraft. He turned away, so he didn't see a man dressed in army camouflage fatigues, wearing a black ski mask and carrying an automatic rifle, emerge from the chopper's side door. The man sprinted a short distance across the ring and grabbed Rigo by his collar. At the same time, two other gunners hopped from the chopper and aimed their rifles into the crowd.

"Get down," Frank yelled, pushing Rosa down behind the seat in front of them.

Joe ducked down, but raised his head just enough to see over the barricade in front of him. He watched as the first gunman dragged Rigo to the helicopter and threw him inside. The other two fired short staccato bursts from their weapons into the air before they dashed back under the whirling blades. The chopper began to rise and turn, kicking up a swirl of reddish dust before it cleared the edge of the stadium and headed out over the city.

Chapter

2

"RIGO!" ROSA'S STRANGLED CRY drew Frank's attention away from the chopper. Glancing around the stadium, Frank saw that most of the crowd appeared to be in shock. Some of them were gazing up at the helicopter, while others were picking themselves up from the ground, where they'd taken cover.

Suddenly a squad of blue-suited police armed with automatic rifles and dressed in riot gear came pouring into the bullring. Another squad surrounded the box where the Hardys were sitting. For a second Joe thought they were being arrested, but when the police pointed their weapons out toward the surrounding crowd, he realized they were protecting Señor Galvan and Rosa.

The leader of the squad shouted, *"Vamos!*

Arriba!" Joe and Frank found themselves encircled by blue uniforms and, along with Rosa and her uncle, hustled out through the crowd.

When they got to the dressing room below the stadium, Rosa burst into tears at the sight of her brother's candles still burning. Señor Galvan went over to comfort her. Over Rosa's shoulder Frank could see the smoldering anger in her uncle's eyes.

To the lieutenant in charge he barked, "Who was that in the helicopter? Where are they taking him?"

"They appeared to be Montañeros, sir," replied the officer. "We will be tracking the helicopter."

"Where are they taking him?"

"We have no idea at this point, sir," the officer said.

"Well, you'd better do your job and find out."

The officer turned toward Joe and Frank. "I'm going to have to ask you boys to leave," he said.

"Ruperto," Rosa said, still teary eyed. "Please. Their names are Joe and Frank Hardy, and they are friends of mine. Let them stay." She turned to Frank. "Please forgive Lieutenant García," she said. "When he's not working as a police officer, he works for Uncle Ramon as a bodyguard. He's very protective of us all."

Frank eyed the handsome Mexican officer, noting that he packed a lot of muscle under his trim-fitting uniform. He was wearing an earphone, discreetly wired under the collar of his shirt to a receiver located on his belt.

García held his finger to the receiver, indicating he was getting a message. A second later he spoke rapidly to one of the members of his squad. All the police except García left the room.

"The helicopter disappeared over the mountains to the south of the city," he said. "There are no sightings of it from our remote units. At least, not yet."

"We should go back to the ranch," Señor Galvan said. "How soon before it's safe to leave?"

"They're clearing the way for your car right now," García said. "We can go. I am sending a guard unit to the ranch ahead of us, just to make sure it's safe there."

As García took Rosa by the arm and led her to the door, she stopped suddenly. "Frank," she said. "I just remembered my Jeep. Could you and Joe drive it to the hacienda for me?"

The Hardys agreed, and after getting directions from Rosa, they were on their way out of town. They drove south through the flat countryside, heading deeper into Mexico. On each side of the highway, the fields were choked with gnarled mesquite trees and prickly pear cactuses.

Frank turned off the highway onto a dusty, unmarked road winding through the fields. A few miles down the road, over the crest of a hill, they found Rancho del Mar, Señor Galvan's hacienda.

"Deluxe," Frank said as he parked the Jeep between a police car and a limousine in the circular driveway lined with tall palm trees. He and Joe stopped for a moment to admire the rambling two-story ranch house of white-washed adobe, its orange tile roof gleaming in the sun. A majestic peacock strolled across the huge green lawn. Nearby a fountain bubbled water into a floating garden of blossoming lily pads.

A housekeeper answered the door and asked them to wait for fifteen or twenty minutes before leading them into a large room with massive wooden ceiling beams and a large fieldstone fireplace. Brightly colored masks and hand-carved wooden animals—lavender frogs, orange dogs with black spots—lent the room a cheerful air while thick, hand-dyed rugs made it feel cozy.

Señor Galvan waited in the study, along with Rosa, Lieutenant García, and a man who introduced himself as Captain Martinez, chief of the Matamoros police.

"We have very little time for formalities,"

Captain Martinez said, "so I'll get right to the point. Frank and Joe Hardy, we have checked on your backgrounds and we found that you have quite a history." He pulled a small notebook out of his shirt pocket and read from it. " 'Cleaning up political corruption in South America, several undercover operations in the U.S.' Seems you have experience all over the Western Hemisphere."

"We know your father is attending a conference on U.S.-Mexico border law enforcement right now," Señor Galvan added. "We are aware of his reputation."

"Did you get our grade point averages, too?" Joe asked.

Frank frowned at his brother and said, "Looks like you ran a pretty thorough check. Mind telling us why?"

"We'd like to make use of your experience during this time of crisis," Galvan began to explain.

"They want you to look after me," Rosa said simply. "They think I can't take care of myself."

"Please, Rosa," Galvan said. "Let me handle this." Turning to the Hardy brothers, he continued, "We thought perhaps you could stay here at Casa del Mar for a few days, provided it's all right with your father. Just until this crisis is over. It would be a double tragedy if anything were to happen to my niece."

16

Frank saw Joe nod yes. "We'd be happy to help out," Frank said.

"With all due respect, Señor Galvan," García said, "are you sure it's necessary to involve two amateurs in this?"

"Actually, it would be extremely useful, Ruperto," Captain Martinez interrupted. "If the young *norteamericanos* are here, that frees you to be elsewhere."

"Yes, sir," García murmured to his superior. He was obviously not pleased with the plan.

Frank and Joe took a few minutes to phone their father, Fenton, the well-known private detective, and let him know where they'd be for the next few days. When they came back, Señor Galvan said, "Welcome to Rancho del Mar. My housekeeper will make you comfortable, and if there's anything you need, please don't hesitate to ask. Now, if you young people will excuse us, we have important work to do to bring Rigo home. Rosa, why don't you show the boys around the ranch before it gets dark?"

Rosa led the Hardys through glass doors at the back of the house and onto a patio filled with banana, orange, and grapefruit trees. Beyond the patio and down a grassy hill Rosa led them to a corral beside the barn.

A wiry old man with white hair and wrinkled skin the color of leather was in the corral. He had a faded, threadbare cape draped across his forearm, and he was talking to two teenage boys in dusty jeans, scuffed basketball shoes, and faded western shirts.

"Who's that?" Frank asked, draping his arms across the top rail of the corral.

"That's El Brujo," Rosa said, an affectionate smile on her face. "He's the one who taught Rigo everything he knows about bullfighting."

As they watched, one of the teenagers walked over to a contraption built on two bicycle wheels set side by side. The horns of a bull had been attached to a sheet of tin metal cut roughly into the shape of a bull's face. Two wheelbarrow handles provided a steering mechanism from the back.

Grasping the handles, the teenager ran the contraption toward El Brujo as if it were a bull. Graceful as a cat, the old man made a pass at the "bull" with his faded cape. All the while, he talked to the aspiring matadors about the moves he was making.

"El Brujo means 'The Magician,'" Rosa said. "Just watch him, and I think you can see why forty years ago he was the greatest bullfighter in Mexico."

"He looks like he could still fight," Frank said, watching El Brujo make a graceful turn with the cape.

After about half an hour, El Brujo and the apprentice bullfighters took a break. Rosa and the Hardys walked over to the old man, who was wiping his face with a red bandanna. "El Brujo," Rosa said. "I want you to meet two friends of mine."

"Con mucho gusto," El Brujo said, bowing slightly and shaking hands with the Hardys. "Any word about Rigo?" he asked in halting English.

Rosa shook her head, focusing on the ground.

"Do you have any idea who might be behind his disappearance?" Joe asked the old man. "Rosa said you two were pretty close."

El Brujo shook his head.

"How about those Montañeros I overheard Lieutenant García mention?" Frank said. "He said those guys in the chopper looked like them. Do you know anything about them?"

El Brujo looked at Frank with a frown and just shook his head again.

"The Montañeros are armed guerrillas fighting for the rights of the peasants and the poor," Rosa said. "They say the government is corrupt and denies them their rights. The government says they are terrorists. They live scattered in the mountains in groups between here and Mexico City. My parents were suspected of being organizers for them."

"So there is a connection," Frank said.

"Rosa!" El Brujo said sharply before letting loose a quick torrent of words in Spanish. Turning to the Hardys, he said, "Forget about

19

the Montañeros. Rigo had nothing to do with them. They are not in the kidnapping business, either."

"So you do know about them," Joe said.

El Brujo was about to say something else, but he was interrupted by Lieutenant García calling to Rosa from the patio. "Rosa, come quick," he said. "We have been contacted by the kidnappers."

Frank and Joe followed her as she sprinted up the hill to the house.

"El Brujo knows something he doesn't want to tell us," Joe said to Frank in a low voice as they entered the house.

"And we're going to have to find out what that is," Frank muttered.

"They want ten million pesos by tomorrow morning," Señor Galvan boomed when Frank and Joe came into the study. "How am I supposed to raise that much money in such a short time?"

"Did they name a drop-off location?" Frank asked.

"No," replied Señor Galvan. "They said they'd call with instructions tomorrow or the day after."

"What about Rigo?" Rosa said. "Is he all right?"

"Listen," Captain Martinez said. He played a tape of the kidnappers' call. The Hardys couldn't understand the rapid-fire Spanish, but they both heard the hard-edged threat in the tone of the voice.

"They say Rigo's unharmed," Rosa translated. "But if they don't get their money, they'll kill him."

"Did you get a trace on the call?" Frank asked Captain Martinez.

The police chief shook his head and said, "Not enough time."

"I've called my banker," Galvan said, "and he's agreed to settle the details tonight. Lieutenant García will come with me. Rosa, make sure you and the boys get a good meal. I'll probably be back after you're in bed." He turned to Frank. "Please take care of my niece."

"You can count on us, Señor Galvan," Frank replied.

At dinner Rosa was despondent. Despite Frank and Joe's efforts to cheer her up, she went to bed after eating only a few bites of her food.

"Let's go check on El Brujo," Joe suggested after Rosa was out of earshot.

"Okay, but we should wait till after her uncle gets back from the bank," Frank said. "We wouldn't want him to come home and find us out of the house."

Joe agreed and they decided to wait until they heard Galvan and García return.

Joe must have dozed off, because he was in

the middle of a dream when Frank shook him awake. The house had fallen silent as Joe followed Frank onto the patio and down the hillside to the barn. The corral was empty. Joe pushed open the barn door, and the Hardys slipped inside.

It took several minutes for their eyes to adjust to the dark. First they made a careful search of the workbench and stalls. Frank was the first to hear the distant sound of a truck's motor disturbing the nighttime stillness. "It's coming this way," he whispered.

Joe paused to listen. "Yep," he replied. "Let's make ourselves scarce." He pointed to a wooden ladder leading up to a hayloft.

Through chinks in the rough wooden floor, they watched as the large double doors at one end of the barn were opened. A diesel truck pulling a large canvas-draped trailer with wooden side slats rumbled into the barn. The driver stepped down from the cab and snapped on a powerful flashlight. It was El Brujo.

The old matador shined his flashlight through the wooden slats of the trailer. From their vantage point, Frank and Joe couldn't see through the canvas roof to determine what the cargo was. Then a bull's horn appeared briefly through an opening between slats and they heard several large beasts snifting on their hooves and snorting nervously.

"Sounds like a lot of them," Joe whispered to Frank.

El Brujo propped the flashlight on a truck tire, opened the trailer's rear gate, and tossed in a couple of heavy bales of hay. Closing and bolting the doors, he retrieved his flashlight and walked to the front of the truck. He raised the hood, checked the oil, wiped the dipstick on his shirt, and closed the hood with a bang.

El Brujo climbed back into the cab and the powerful engine roared to life. As the truck started to pull out of the barn, Frank and Joe hurried to the opening into the hayloft to get a better look.

Out of the corner of his eye, Joe noticed a large, dark shape fall from the rafters of the barn. No, it didn't fall—it flew. Spreading its wings, it was going for Joe's head. An ear-piercing screech and a flash of razor-sharp talons caused Joe to duck, then lose his balance.

He groped for Frank, for the edge of the loft, for anything he could grip. It was too late, though, and he plunged through the opening into the darkness.

Chapter

3

FRANK SAW HIS BROTHER fall as a huge barn owl flapped past his head, brushing his ear with its wing feathers. He saw Joe land on top of the canvas tarp covering the long trailer as it pulled out of the barn with increasing speed.

Joe heard the metal grommets at the edge of the canvas tear when he landed, but the fastenings held. As the truck picked up speed, it hit a rut in the road, jouncing him up into the air. When he came down again he heard the fastenings rip a little further.

Thinking about the sharp horns of the bulls below him, Joe realized he would be in real trouble if the canvas gave way. He considered jumping off, but the truck was already moving too fast.

Like a beetle, Joe scuttled on his stomach toward the rear of the canvas roof. Carefully he peered over the edge and saw that the slatted doors didn't reach all the way up to the canvas. There was a gap big enough to crawl through. Catching a whiff of the earthy smell inside, he hesitated. Was it better to travel on a canvas roof, risking a ride without anything to cling to, or to climb down into a dark trailer with a few bad-tempered bulls? His decision was made for him when a second bump sent him two feet up into the air. This time when he landed the canvas ripped away from its fastenings and he dropped down into the truck.

He must have hit one of the bulls on its massive flank before getting wedged against the wall. The bull snorted in surprise and turned his low-slung head around to look at Joe.

"Easy, pal," Joe said, struggling to his feet in the tiny space between the bull's haunches and the slats of the trailer wall. Over the din of the whining tires and the truck's motor, he wasn't sure if the animal heard him. "Nice bull," he said anyway, patting the wall of hair and muscle that pressed him against the wall and keeping an eye on the gleaming horns protruding from the bull's head.

When Frank saw his brother plastered like a fly on top of the trailer, he had only one thought: Follow that vehicle. He flew down the ladder and landed hard on the barn's hay-covered floor. He sprinted after the truck, but it was already moving too fast. As the sound of the engine faded and the taillights disappeared in the dark, Frank slowed to a jog. He hoped to see Joe walking back to the barn, a sheepish grin on his face, telling him how he'd somersaulted off the truck and El Brujo had never even seen him. But long after the red taillights winked out in the darkness, there was no Joe.

He waited longer than he should have. In the silence of the Mexican night, he heard the first songbird of the morning, and already a faint blue glow was rising over the eastern horizon. Walking back to the house, he thought about waking Señor Galvan or seeking help from Ruperto García. Neither idea appealed to him. But he was sure Rosa would help him find out where the truck was headed. He walked through the silent yard until he stood beneath Rosa's bedroom window. He tossed a few pebbles against the glass. First he saw a light, then Rosa appeared, blinking away sleep.

Frank motioned for her to come down. A few minutes later she joined him in the yard. She was barefoot and wearing a white robe. Her black hair hung down to her waist. She and Frank walked over to the pool. Frank explained about Joe's fall onto the truck.

"What were you doing in the barn in the middle of the night?" Rosa asked.

"We wanted to check on El Brujo," Frank said. "We thought he was acting kind of suspicious this afternoon."

"I see," said Rosa coolly. "And this must be done by moonlight? You Americans have strange habits."

"I could say the same about you Mexicans," Frank said testily. "Like taking a load of bulls out for a ride in the middle of the night."

It was getting lighter, and Frank could see Rosa's face, glowing in the pink light of the dawn. Her expression was full of concern. "El Brujo is very devoted to my family," she continued. "If he does know something about Rigo, he would say. You don't have to sneak around to find that out."

"Rosa, I've got to find out where that truck is headed—and *soon.*"

"Uncle Ramon sells bulls all over Mexico. That truck could be headed anywhere—Chihuahua, Guadalajara, down south around Cuernavaca." She paused for a moment. "I'll tell you what," she said finally. "At breakfast I'll find out from Uncle Ramon where El Brujo has gone. He wouldn't be very happy to know you were sneaking around at night, so I'll leave that part out."

"Okay," Frank said. "I guess that's the best we can do for now."

At the front of the trailer, past the mammoth humps of the bulls jammed between the boxlike walls of the trailer, Joe spotted a shelf. If he could make it there, he could perch above the horns and hooves of the shifting animals.

Gripping the slatted wall, Joe found a foothold and pulled himself up higher than the heads of the bulls. He inched along the wall, managing to reach the shelf without harm, although he could see many pairs of dark, glittering eyes watching from the dark.

Once he'd reached the shelf, he sat down, leaning back against the front wall of the trailer and taking a deep breath. He massaged his cramped fingers. He was safe, at least for a while.

It didn't take long for the steady roar of the engine and the vibration of the road to lull Joe to sleep. How long he slept, he didn't know, but the gearing down of the engine jarred him awake. The sun was coming up, and he could see the bulls more clearly. They were huge, he realized, and in the light of day their bulging eyes were bloodshot and mean-looking.

Joe felt the truck jolt off the pavement onto a rutted, unpaved road. Choking dust filled the inside of the trailer. The bulls bellowed and butted one another in the rocking truck. Joe hung on to the trailer's wooden slats so he wouldn't fall into the bulls. Through the slats he could see rough, dry countryside. Prickly pear and tall stands of cactuses and hardy mesquite bushes grew among piles of rock. It was getting hot.

The truck came to a stop. With the motor off and the dust settling, the bulls calmed down. Joe could hear the ticking of the motor as it cooled off. Through the wooden slats, Joe saw El Brujo step down from the cab of the truck, stretch his arms into the air, then bend over and touch his toes. He stood up straight and greeted someone. *"Buenos días,"* he heard a male voice reply, but before Joe could see who it was, a shaft of sunlight arced into the dusty gloom of the trailer. The bulls, desperate to escape their prison on wheels, stampeded out of the rear door and down a ramp, leaving the trailer empty.

Joe glanced around quickly. Noticing the shelf he was sitting on was actually the cover of a large feed bin, Joe gripped the handle, lifted the lid, and slipped into the bin. It was dark and hot inside. Steel rods and hard metal cases jabbed at his back. He felt around with his hands, guessing that he was lying on top of tools, but as his eyes adjusted he saw that El Brujo wasn't making any ordinary bull delivery. He could see machine guns, ammunition boxes, rifles, plastic explosives—Joe was lying in a box full of military hardware.

He held up a shiny new TEC-DC9 automatic loader. Just as he was checking for ammunition, the lid opened, and bright sunlight blinded him for a moment. He heard a gasp of surprise, and when he squinted up, he was staring at three grim-faced men. The stubby, black barrels of three DC9s grazed his throat.

Someone spoke in Spanish behind them. Joe couldn't translate.

One of the men handed his gun to his partner, reached into the bin, and grabbed Joe by the collar. He jerked him out of the bin and sent him sprawling on the filth-covered floor.

"Hey," Joe said angrily, standing and rubbing the back of his head. "Take it easy."

A short, stocky man in army fatigues stood in front of Joe. Although he wasn't much older than Joe, he appeared older because of his handlebar mustache and thick black eyebrows, which were lowered in a frown over small, beadlike eyes. One of the men behind Joe said in broken English so Joe could understand, "Comandante Zeta, Yankee had gun."

"I was just looking at it," Joe protested. "I wasn't going to—"

"Shut up!" ordered Zeta. Speaking to one of his men, he said, "Get El Brujo, pronto!"

The guard left. Zeta headed out the back of the truck. A gun at his back prompted Joe to follow. Outside, Zeta ordered his men to tie Joe's hands and feet with leather thongs.

Joe saw a corral with perhaps a dozen men and women standing beside it. They all wore ragged fatigues, leather sandals, and floppy straw hats. Their chests were crisscrossed with ammunition belts bristling with bullets.

Some of them seemed to be barely in their teens. All were armed with either guns or machetes, the long, lethal blades gleaming in the sun. From their army fatigues, Joe guessed they were Montañeros.

Thinking quickly, Joe said to Zeta, "Look, I think I can help you. If I could just see that Rigo is all right, then I'm sure Señor Galvan would pay any amount of ransom . . ." His voice trailed off. Zeta was glaring at him, and Joe realized he'd made a tactical error. The hatred in Zeta's predatory eyes made Joe's insides turn to jelly.

"You know too much," Zeta growled.

He shouted something in Spanish that Joe didn't understand. Then four Montañeros lined up about ten feet from Joe, and Zeta ordered *"Listos!"* in a loud voice. The gunmen raised their weapons and aimed them at Joe's heart. Joe was facing a firing squad.

He had never felt so helpless, bound hand and foot, gazing down the barrels of four rifles. *"Apunte!"* Zeta ordered. The soldiers cocked their weapons. Joe stared in disbelief. He wanted to say something, anything, but no words would come. How could they execute him when they hadn't questioned him first? He wished he'd never opened his mouth about Rigo.

The man they called Comandante Zeta lifted his right arm, ready to give his final command.

Chapter

4

JOE STARED WIDE-EYED down the four gun barrels pointed at his chest. Zeta was about to give the "fire" command when El Brujo silently appeared and stepped between Joe and the guns.

Speaking rapidly in Spanish, El Brujo managed to convince Comandante Zeta to order the executioners to lower their weapons. Joe caught the words *Rosa Galvan* and *amigo,* the latter meaning "friend," mentioned several times.

The guards unceremoniously tied Joe to the fence of the corral, next to some horses. El Brujo continued to talk to Zeta while the Montañeros unloaded the weapons from the feed bin in the truck. They strapped the hardware on to two pack mules tethered among the horses, cinching the ropes tight.

When they were finished, Zeta shook hands with El Brujo and mounted his horse. He paused for one more glance at Joe. His steady eyes had no hint of humor in them, but his lips formed a half smile.

He turned his horse, called the other Montañeros to saddle up, and soon the band of revolutionaries trotted off in a ragged line toward the rocky, juniper-spotted hills.

El Brujo turned to Joe, who was still tied to the fence. "Who are you, really?" he asked. "Why were you in my truck with the bulls?" He shoved his weathered face just inches from Joe's—so close that Joe could smell his breath.

"I'm just . . . you know," Joe said. "I'm just a friend of Rosa's."

"No," El Brujo said, pulling a seven-inch blade from inside his shirt. "You will tell me the truth, one way or another."

The knife blade was polished like chrome, and its tip, Joe could see, was needle-sharp. Joe wasn't sure what El Brujo was going to do with it until he brought it down to where his wrists were bound. Then, with a deft twist of the blade, he severed the thongs. Joe rubbed his skin where the leather had pinched the flesh, watching as El Brujo kneeled down to cut the bonds at his ankles.

"I guess I should say thanks," Joe said. "You saved my life."

"Get in the truck," El Brujo told Joe gruffly.

Joe climbed into the cab, and soon they were on the highway again, heading north.

El Brujo drove in stony silence. The highway stretched in front of them all the way to the horizon, slicing through the vast, scrub-brush plain like a black ribbon.

"I really meant what I said," Joe said. "I would have been dead if you hadn't stepped in."

El Brujo nodded but didn't respond right away. Then, after several minutes of silence, El Brujo glanced away from the road. "You young men are always foolish. Like the young bulls before they have the wisdom of years, you look for more trouble than you can handle."

Joe felt a little guilty. "Hey, it was an accident, okay? I fell onto your truck." Joe explained how the owl caused him to fall from the hayloft onto the truck late the night before.

A hint of a smile creased the old man's brown, wrinkled face. "I might have known," he mused.

"What do you mean?" Joe asked.

After a moment's hesitation El Brujo said, "That owl is a friend of mine, and it seems he was trying to tell you something."

For a second, Joe thought the old man might be a little off his rocker, but he decided to play along anyway. "What do you think the owl was trying to tell me?" he asked.

"How would I know?" El Brujo said, chuckling. "I wasn't there."

A little while later Joe asked, "What's that guy Zeta going to do with all those weapons?"

"I will tell you," El Brujo said. "But only because the owl and the bulls seem to think you are trustworthy." He glanced skeptically at Joe. "Although I must say I don't see why."

Joe said, "Oh, the bulls talk to you, too?"

El Brujo glanced calmly at Joe. "It's what they *didn't* say that reveals their trust."

"And what *didn't* they say?" Joe continued.

"That you should die" came the reply. "At least not yet. That's why I stopped Zeta from killing you."

Joe felt a bit foolish. The old man was like an impish jester who liked to set traps with his riddles. Joe had a hard time understanding the old man's accent and wondered about his intentions.

As the truck barreled along the highway, El Brujo explained to Joe that the Montañeros were poor farmers whose land had been taken from them by wealthy landowners. The police, under orders from the president, had forced the Montañeros off land that had been in their families for generations. Homeless, scrounging for food, living in the high desert, they believed they had no choice but to take up arms against the government.

"Did they kidnap Rigo?"

"No," El Brujo said. "They would never harm Rigo. The Montañeros think of Rosa's parents as martyrs for their cause. They believe both Rigo and Rosa should be left alone, even though Señor Galvan himself owns land that belongs to some of them."

"What about the guns?" Joe said. "What will Zeta do with all those weapons you just delivered?"

"No more questions, boy," said the old man. "The road is very long, and you wear me out with all your talk. Besides, you must be getting sleepy."

"No," Joe said, stifling a yawn. "I'm not tired at all. I want to know where all those guns are coming from."

"Forget about the guns," murmured El Brujo. "Forget about the Montañeros." A strange, lilting tone had crept into his voice, blending into the smooth whine of the tires on the pavement. Joe slouched down in his seat, feeling the vibration of the truck's chassis. The last thing he said before slipping into a deep sleep was "El Brujo. Didn't Rosa say that means, 'The Wizard'?"

"Yes," said the old man. "That's what it means."

"Don't bother me with questions about business, Rosa—not now," said Señor Galvan, obviously annoyed. Frank and Rosa had joined her uncle for a late breakfast on the patio under the banana trees at Rancho del Mar. "The shipment of bulls is the furthest thing from my mind."

"But, Uncle Ramon," Rosa said. "I was just wondering when El Brujo would return."

"Probably late this afternoon," he replied. Frank had to admire Rosa's persistence as she tried to persuade her uncle to reveal where El Brujo had gone with the truck—and with Joe, Frank hoped.

Lieutenant García stood close by in his *policía* uniform, sipping coffee with milk from an oversize mug. "Señor Galvan, when the kidnappers call," he said, "be sure to keep them on the line as long as possible."

Galvan nodded. "Of course. Let's just hope your equipment can trace the call this time. It makes me nervous, having all that cash here in the house."

"What could be safer?" García replied. "We have the place well guarded, not to mention the hidden surveillance team stationed at the ranch perimeter. Not even an army would be foolish enough to go for the money here."

Frank said, "Where do you think the exchange will take place?"

"Hard to say," García replied. "The Montañeros keep to the countryside, rarely coming into the cities."

"Really?" Frank said. "Why would they kidnap Rigo in such a public way yesterday?"

"Perhaps they are changing from guerrilla tactics to terrorist ones," García said. "In any case, Rigo's gone, and until we can ensure his safety, it's pointless to ask why."

The housekeeper came out on the patio, interrupting their discussion. "Excuse me," she said to Galvan, "but Señor Stanley is here to see you."

Galvan grimaced, muttering, "What does *he* want?" as he stood up. "I've got to see about some business," he told the others. García started to follow, but Galvan said, "No, thank you, Ruperto. This is private." The he disappeared into the house, heading toward his study.

Galvan's manner seemed too abrupt to Frank, and he wondered what sort of private business could be more important than his nephew's kidnapping. On an impulse, Frank excused himself from the table to go to the bathroom.

After passing through the living room, he crept up to the study doors and pressed his ear against the hardwood surface.

He heard a booming voice with a Texas accent saying, "My friends down at the bank tell me of a big withdrawal. You're the only one with that kind of money around here."

"Yes," Galvan said coldly. "What of it?"

"I sure do hope it's for me," said the man the housekeeper had called Stanley.

"No, it is for another matter," Galvan said.

"You mean that little abduction yesterday?" the Texan asked.

A brief pause almost caused Frank's heart to skip a beat. What if Galvan were to open the study doors right then? He was relieved when he heard Galvan say, "What do you know about that?"

"That's the ten-million-peso question, ain't it?" the Texan said. His voice grew hard. "I ain't playing any games here, Galvan. Looks like you're being pulled two ways at once, and I'm just making sure I get my piece."

"Is that all you have to say, Stanley?" Galvan's words were clipped. "Because I intend to live up to my obligations. Yes, I did withdraw that money, but it is not for you. You will get yours as soon as our contract has been fulfilled."

Frank knew the conversation was just about over, so he hurried back to the patio to join Rosa and Lieutenant García. He was glad he did, because just as he sat back down they heard the big study door slam shut. From the patio the three of them watched Stanley's white Cadillac squeal out of the driveway.

"I'll be with Señor Galvan," García said, leaving the patio. "We need to discuss our strategy for dealing with the next call from the kidnappers."

"Who was that?" Frank asked when García had gone.

"Ray Don Stanley," she said, gazing down the road at the Cadillac, which was heading north toward the U.S. border. "He's a gun merchant, the biggest in South Texas. He comes out here a lot, because Uncle Ramon likes to hunt. During deer season Ray Don brings American hunting parties to the ranch. In case you didn't guess, he's not one of my favorite people."

"That's interesting," Frank said. "Does he sell helicopters, too?"

Rosa sat up straight in her chair. "What are you getting at?"

Frank briefly explained what he'd overheard at the study door.

Rosa's eyes widened. "You shouldn't have done that," she said. "Uncle Ramon is very protective of his privacy in business."

"That may be," Frank said. "But it looks like privacy doesn't mean much to Ray Don Stanley. His friends down at the bank were pretty willing to divulge confidential information to Stanley about your uncle." An idea was forming at the back of Frank's mind. "How would you like to show me Ray Don's store?" he asked.

"Frank," Rosa said with a tinge of excitement in her voice. "Are you asking me to do a little detective work with you?"

"I guess I am," he said. "You seem like you could handle it."

"Thank you, Frank," she said. "My uncle and Ruperto treat me as if I were a little girl to be shielded from everything that matters."

"I doubt they'll be thrilled by the idea of your poking around in Ray Don's business," Frank said.

"I'll tell them I have to pick up something from the surf shop," Rosa said as they got up and went into Galvan's study.

Lieutenant García, who was sitting with Galvan, listened to Rosa's proposition and quickly said, "This is foolishness. There is nothing important enough at the shop for you to risk your life. What if the kidnappers want to up the ante by taking you, too?"

"I'll be with her the whole time," Frank said. "Besides, I seriously doubt they'd cross the border and risk another kidnapping in broad daylight."

Galvan considered for a moment, then said, "Three hours. That's it. You be back in three hours."

"Don't worry, *tío*," Rosa said, giving her uncle a light kiss on the cheek. "We'll be back before sunset."

Stanley's store was located in a strip mall near a suburban development about five miles north of the border. A pair of Texas longhorns were mounted above the front door. As they pulled into the parking lot, Rosa and Frank saw Stanley's Cadillac parked in front, along with several dozen other trucks and four-wheel-drive vehicles. "Bingo," Frank said. "The cowboy's home."

"Park around back," Rosa said. "And you go in. Stanley knows me and my Jeep."

Frank did as Rosa suggested. Once inside, he glanced around the brightly lit weapons supermarket. It was crowded with men, women, even children, strolling aisles that offered every type of gun and ammunition imaginable. Stanley was behind the counter, still wearing his wide-brimmed western hat.

"Need some help, son?" he asked in his rumbling Texas voice when Frank walked up to the counter.

"I'd like to do a little plinking out on my friend's ranch," Frank said. "You know, target practice. I'm in the market for a machine gun."

Stanley looked into Frank's eyes for a moment, assessing him with a critical eye. Then a chuckle rumbled up from deep inside his throat. He walked around the counter and draped an arm across Frank's shoulder.

"You know as well as I do, little buddy, that selling machine guns is illegal in the U.S., but I'll tell you what I'll do." He brought his face close to Frank's and grinned. "You got enough cash, and I'll sell you a semiautomatic and a

43

conversion kit. You take it home, and presto, you got your very own little machine gun. What do you say?"

"Sound's good," Frank said, easing out from under Stanley's big arm. "I have what you might call a delicate question. Let's say I want to buy some guns here and take them into Mexico. How would I do that?"

Ray Don looked into Frank's eyes again, apparently sizing him up. Again he chuckled. "You ain't kiddin', are you, partner? Well, let me tell you something. You flash a little cash, and it's like that guy on TV says: 'Come on down!' All kinds of doors open up."

Frank was staring past Stanley's shoulder down an aisle full of revolvers. His stomach lurched when he saw Rosa step briefly into view. She motioned nervously to him, then stepped behind a display full of holsters and rifle bags.

Thinking quickly, Frank said, "Hey, thanks. I'm going to have to think about it."

"What's to think about?" Stanley said. "We got easy credit payment plans. Heck, I'll even throw in a little deal sweetener if you buy in bulk."

Backing away with a wave of his hand, Frank said, "Thanks again. I'll be in touch." He hustled down the aisle. When he spotted Rosa, he said, "I thought you—"

"Ruperto's here," she said. "Quick, hide."

Chapter

5

FRANK DUCKED BEHIND THE DISPLAY where Rosa was crouched. Then he sneaked a peek back up the aisle. At first he didn't recognize García because he wasn't in uniform.

Garcia was approaching Stanley, who was back behind his counter. Frank saw the two men shake hands. Then García turned to check back down the aisle behind him. Frank quickly ducked back again, but wasn't sure if he'd been spotted.

"Let's get out of here, Rosa," Frank said. "He may have seen me."

They stood up, turned their backs, and walked straight to the door. As they got into Rosa's Jeep, Frank said, "What do you think García's doing here?"

"I don't know," Rosa said. "We might find out if we wait and follow him."

"You're catching on to this game pretty fast," Frank said. At Frank's suggestion, Rosa drove out of the lot and parked her Jeep behind a warehouse across the street. Frank kept watch, and before long Stanley and García walked out to their cars, got in, and drove off in a line down the boulevard. Frank and Rosa followed the two cars at a safe distance. García was driving one of the pickup trucks from Rancho del Mar.

"I'll bet it's the money," Frank said as they drove. "Maybe your uncle is ready to pay off his debt to Stanley and he sent García."

"Or maybe Ruperto's investigating Ray Don because he thinks he knows something about Rigo," Rosa said.

They followed the two cars into the warehouse district of South Padre's industrial waterfront. The air smelled of dead fish, petrolcum, and decay. Docks built on wooden pilings stretched out over the water on one side of the street, some of them supporting warehouses, while crumbling storage sheds and abandoned buildings lined the other.

Stanley parked in front of a large, rusty metal structure, and García pulled up beside him. Frank parked the Jeep a block away, behind a bread-delivery truck. They watched the Texas gun dealer lead García into the warehouse.

"Let's go," Frank said. "Just be careful to stay out of sight."

They got out of the Jeep and crossed the street. Staying close to the warehouse wall, they made their way to where Stanley had entered the building. The door was locked. Frank checked the street in both directions to make sure no one was watching. Then he pulled out his plastic-laminated student ID card and jimmied the latch with it.

Quietly they slipped into the darkened warehouse. An oily smell greeted them. "What is that?" Rosa whispered, scrunching her nose at the acrid odor.

"Guns," Frank said, peering into an open crate. He looked down an aisle of similarly labeled crates. "Lots and lots of guns."

Using the crates as cover, they slipped toward the open doors at the back of the building. They took cover behind a stack of coiled razor wire. From there they could see a dockside loading area. Lashed to the dock was a forty-foot shrimp boat with its deck hatches open.

Off to the left, near a glass-enclosed office, Ray Don Stanley and Lieutenant Ruperto García were talking to a man in a battered sea captain's cap. The man had a lighted cigarette dangling from the corner of his mouth. Rosa whispered, "That's Captain Cisneros. He manages the fleet of shrimping boats my uncle owns."

"Looks like he's catching more than just shrimp," Frank replied. The men were engaged in a heated discussion. "I'm going to see if I can get close enough to hear," Frank said. "You wait here."

He ducked back down the aisle of gun-loaded crates and doubled back a few rows nearer, creeping up to within eight feet of Stanley, García, and Captain Cisneros. Pressing his back up against the crates, Frank listened carefully.

"Yes, sir," Stanley was saying, clapping García on the back. "Me and Captain Cisneros here are gonna make a stash of cash on this shipment. If you ask me, Galvan is stupid for arming the Montañeros when they just turn around and kidnap his nephew, but that's his business—and yours, I guess."

"Do you know where the Montañeros are keeping Rigo?" García asked.

"Nope," Stanley said. "Nobody can keep track of those desert rats. It's creepy the way they appear and disappear. All I know is where to drop off the shipments. And where my money comes from."

"Obviously Señor Galvan wants to know where the Montañeros took his nephew," said García. "But why do you think he's supplying arms to them?"

"I thought you just said you were his business partner," Stanley said.

"I did" came the reply. "But—"

"Then if you don't already know, ask him yourself," the Texan said. "Like I said, I think it's stupid, but don't you go telling him I said that. Now let's go check on Captain Cisnero's manifest. I don't want anything going wrong with this shipment."

The three went back into the office. Frank returned to where Rosa was hiding, crouched behind her, and whispered, "Did you know your uncle was arming the Montañeros?"

"I had no idea," Rosa said. Frank told her what he'd heard, and Rosa said, "But the Montañeros are fighting against wealthy men like my uncle."

"Could he be helping them to get revenge against the government for your parents' deaths?" Frank asked.

"He could," she said, "but he'd have to keep the whole thing secret from his business partners and the *policía.*"

"Lieutenant García didn't seem to know about it," Frank said. "Until now."

"But why would the Montañeros turn around and kidnap Rigo?" Rosa wondered.

"It doesn't make sense, does it?" Frank said. "After all, you don't go around biting the hand that feeds you."

An edge of fear crept into Rosa's voice.

"Now that Ruperto knows, he'll turn my uncle in to the *policía.*"

Frank said, "I doubt it," glancing over his shoulder to see if the three men were still in the office. "I'm beginning to think that García is up to something other than just protecting your uncle. Maybe he's got some kind of deal going with Stanley." He glanced at his watch. "Which reminds me. We have a deal to keep, and we ought to be getting back or we'll be late."

"No, not yet," Rosa said. "Now that we've come this far, let's check the boat. Maybe we can find some clues about Rigo. Maybe they're holding him here."

"I doubt it," Frank said. "But at least we can try to find out where that rust-bucket is headed. Maybe that'll lead us to Rigo."

Keeping the crates between them and the corner office, Frank and Rosa moved over to the dock. Frank checked that the coast was clear before gripping Rosa's hand and running across the dock with her. They leaped onto the deck of the shrimp boat and crouched behind the motor for the trawling winch.

It was a well-worn vessel with the name SS *Mosquito* painted on its bow. There were ropes and heavy nets hanging all over the deck. It smelled of gasoline, spoiling shrimp, and human sweat. A wild-looking cat scampered across the deck, startling both Rosa and Frank.

Frank glanced down into the holding tank, where he saw stacks of heavy wooden crates. He assumed they held more guns and ammo. They climbed into the pilot house where a cup of cold coffee rested on charts of Gulf fishing areas. Propped in the corner was a high-powered rifle.

"They don't need that for catching shrimp," Frank commented. He started to study the maps spread out on the navigator's table.

"Uh-oh," Rosa said. Frank saw Captain Cisneros and two of his crew members jumping onto the boat. Ray Don Stanley and García stood on the dock, casting off the lines.

They ducked down below the level of the window and crawled out the door of the pilot house, taking refuge under an overturned lifeboat.

It was stifling under the lifeboat, and the stench of rotten shrimp was strong. Frank felt the boat's engines rumble to life. Through a small crack between the lifeboat and the deck, they could see that the shrimp boat was pulling away from the dock.

Minutes later, as the heavily laden boat began to pitch in the swells of the outer harbor, Frank and Rosa listened for footsteps near their hiding place. Hearing none, Frank peeked under the rim to get some idea of where they were headed. In the gathering darkness, the lights of South Padre receded.

By keeping his eye on the coast, he figured they were heading southeast.

"Could we toss this lifeboat into the water and make a run for it?" Rosa whispered.

Frank shook his head. "Cisneros would spot us. Remember that rifle we saw up in the pilot house? These guys are probably the kind to shoot first and ask questions later."

Within twenty minutes, the sky was completely dark and the city lights were little more than pinpoints of light sparkling on the horizon. Suddenly the captain cut the throttle, leaving the shrimp boat idle in the water. A powerful beam of light bathed the boat in a harsh glare. Frank could hear the sound of another boat motor off the starboard side. There was an excited voice coming from behind the spotlight.

Squinting in the light, Frank made out a gunmetal gray boat with the word *policia* painted in white block letters on the bow. A Spanish voice over a loudspeaker issued an order to Captain Cisneros. "He said, 'We're coming aboard,' " Rosa whispered.

The police boat pulled alongside the SS *Mosquito*. A man in a police uniform stepped aboard. He shook hands with Captain Cisneros. The men talked for a few minutes, then the officer waved two of his men aboard the *Mosquito*. They climbed into the hold, and a few minutes later the sound of the hydraulic winch broke the silence. A crate of weapons emerged from the hold, and the arm of the loader swung it out over the water to the police boat.

As Frank watched the loading operations, his mind was racing. If the weapons were intended for the Montañeros, as Stanley had suggested, then why were they being delivered to the police? Perhaps, he reasoned, the police boat was skimming a little off the top in exchange for letting the shrimp boat pass the border without a hassle.

His suspicion was confirmed when Captain Cisneros burst out of the pilot house and shouted, "No more. That's enough!"

The police officer argued with the captain, shoving him and then laughing when the captain lay sprawled on the deck. Cisneros rose and took a swing at the uniformed officer, but the man ducked, countering with an uppercut that sent Cisneros back to the deck. They wrestled, kicking and scrambling, until the officer broke free. He deftly leaped off the shrimp boat and onto his own boat, which gunned its motors and pulled away.

Cisneros shook his fist at the police boat and then raced up to the pilot house. Seconds later Frank and Rosa heard the unmistakable crack of rifle shots above their heads.

"Don't move," Frank said to Rosa, as he flattened himself to the deck. He heard the

thunk of a heavy metal object hitting the lifeboat. When it rolled into view, Frank saw it
was a grenade. Without a second's hesitation,
he scrambled to his knees and kicked the grenade so it skittered across the deck and disappeared into the open storage hold belowdecks
where the crates of munitions were stored.

Bracing his shoulders against the boat above
him, Frank lifted it enough so that Rosa could
scoot out.

"Dive," he shouted, and she leaped over the
side of the boat. Frank followed a second later,
just as the grenade detonated.

Chapter

6

AN INSTANT AFTER the grenade exploded, the munitions crates in the hold ignited and the shrimp boat blew apart.

The explosion catapulted Frank twenty feet before he slammed into the water. Salty brine flooded his nose and mouth. When he surfaced, sputtering and coughing, he saw what remained of the flaming, hissing *Mosquito* sinking beneath the waves.

"Rosa!" he shouted before he saw the police boat plowing through the waves, heading in the opposite direction. Apparently they didn't hear his feeble shout over the sound of their motors, for the boat was soon out of sight.

Could they have captured Rosa? he thought. One look at the wreckage of the SS *Mosquito* convinced Frank there was no point looking for Captain Cisneros and his crew.

"Frank!" Rosa shouted. "Are you all right?" Frank had almost forgotten Rosa was a strong swimmer. He saw her bobbing in the water behind him. He swam toward her, grabbing on to a large, jagged piece of wood that floated nearby.

"I thought you were dead," she said.

"Nope," Frank said. "Just wet.

"Me, too," she said. "And cold."

"Let's keep moving," he said. Holding tight to their makeshift wooden raft, they began kicking their feet. "We should be able to stay warm this way."

Slowly, they moved toward the shore and the twinkling lights of South Padre.

"Estamos aquí," El Brujo said, shaking Joe awake. "We're here." He stopped the truck at the dirt road leading to Rancho del Mar. Joe climbed down from the truck, and El Brujo drove it down toward the equipment sheds behind the barn.

Joe looked up at the velvet-black sky and a million stars. Dead tired, he began to walk up the driveway to the hacienda, which gleamed white in the moonlight. He had much to think about as he trudged along. El Brujo had refused to answer his questions about the weapons delivery, but Joe was sure he knew more than he was letting on. Most important of all, he had denied the Montañeros were involved in Rigo's kidnapping. Was he lying? All his mumbo-jumbo about owls and bulls trying to convey a message to Joe suggested that El Brujo was capable of saying—or believing—almost anything.

He couldn't puzzle it out. He walked into the yard and gazed up at the house. He was glad to see a light in the window of his and Frank's room. He was hoping that Frank had uncovered some useful evidence. He was also anxious to tell his brother that there were weapons involved in this case, lots of them. So far, he didn't know if they were connected to Rigo's disappearance, but Joe couldn't believe it was just a coincidence.

The house was dark and silent. Joe climbed the stairs and walked down the hall to his room. The door was open.

"Frank," he called, but there was no answer. As he stepped into the room, someone grabbed him from behind in a choke hold. He could feel a hard metal object—probably the barrel of a pistol—being jabbed into his lower back. Then he heard Lieutenant García's voice say, "Where are they, you little punk? Tell me or I'll beat you to a pulp."

Joe stood still as stone. A second voice said, "Bring him down to the study."

García shoved Joe ahead of him, steering

57

him back down the stairs and into Galvan's study. García's boss, Captain Martinez, followed them into the room. Joe turned to García and said, "The next time you jump me from behind, you'd better watch yourself."

Joe saw a grim smile of satisfaction flash across the lieutenant's face. "That's just a taste of what's to come if you don't tell us where Rosa is," García said.

"Rosa's missing?" Joe said. "What about Frank?"

"Don't play stupid with us, boy," Martinez said. "Tell us where they are, now. Tell us who you are and who you're working for."

"I don't know where they are," Joe said. "I didn't even know they were missing. And I'm not working for anyone." He glanced at García. "Where's Señor Galvan? He'll back me up on this."

"He knows only what you told him," García said coldly. "Señor Galvan cannot help you this time, not with both Rosa and Rigo gone. He has authorized me to arrest you if you do not cooperate. If you have not seen your brother, tell us where you have been the last twenty-four hours."

"He was with me," said a quiet voice from the door of the study. "Is there a problem?"

Joe looked up to see El Brujo, still wearing his dusty work clothes. He stood at the door, his fingers nervously twisting the sweat-stained straw hat in his hands. "We were transporting the bulls to Rancho Sonora."

"Rosa has been missing for over nine hours," García said. "She promised to be back in three. She went to South Padre with Frank Hardy."

El Brujo's eyes grew wide with concern. "Has she been kidnapped, too?" he said.

"We don't know yet," Captain Martinez said. "When the young American was with you, did he make any phone calls or do anything else unusual?"

El Brujo shook his head. "It was a routine delivery. The boy slept all the way back."

Joe was thinking that the weapons delivery and his near-execution were hardly what he would call routine. He decided not to challenge El Brujo at that moment, but he promised himself he would do it later.

"We can put him under arrest for suspicion, but I don't see what good it will do," Captain Martinez said to Lieutenant García. "If your cattle man is telling the truth, then the boy cannot know where Rosa is."

"I speak the truth," El Brujo said to García. "The boy was with me."

"I'm sorry to have wasted your time, sir," García said to Martinez.

"Don't worry about it, Lieutenant," replied Martinez. "We have units searching for Rosa in Matamoros, and the South Padre police are cooperating. We'll find them." Removing a card from his wallet, he handed it to Joe. "If you hear from your brother, give me a call immediately."

Joe stood up to leave, but García stopped him. "Why did you go with El Brujo? You and your brother both promised to keep an eye on Rosa."

"Maybe I thought it would be educational," he replied. "Maybe I'm thinking about taking up bullfighting someday."

García answered with a steely gaze. "Next time, Mr. Joe Hardy, you check with me before trying to involve yourself with ranch business," he said.

Meanwhile, Frank and Rosa were paddling their piece of shrimp boat wreckage through the surf off South Padre Island. The current had swept them back north of the border. When their feet finally touched the sandy bottom, they dragged themselves onto dry land and noticed the beach was deserted. It was very late.

Once she had caught her breath, Rosa said, "The warehouse district isn't far from here. Maybe a mile up the beach."

"I guess we start walking," Frank said. Checking his pockets, he drew out a soggy wallet and keys to the Jeep. "At least I didn't lose these," he said, attempting to sound cheerful.

He looked over at Rosa, who was shivering. "Let's go. We'll be there in no time."

When they finally got to the Jeep, Frank found an old wool poncho. He wrapped it around Rosa before starting back to the ranch.

"I'd better call my uncle," Rosa said. "He must be worried."

Rosa picked up the cellular phone and dialed. She talked briefly with her uncle in Spanish. After she hung up, Frank asked, "What did you tell him?"

"The truth," she answered. Then, sheepishly, she said, "But not the whole truth. Not about the explosion and our—our swim. But everything else."

"What did he say?" Frank asked.

"Only that I should never have placed myself in danger like that. He seemed pretty angry."

"Did he explain why he's paying Ray Don Stanley to ship arms to the Montañeros?" Frank said.

"No," she replied. "He cut me short and said we could talk about whatever we saw when we got back to the ranch. He said he just wants us back as soon as possible."

When Frank and Rosa pulled up to the hacienda, they could see a tinge of dawn behind the mesa to the east. Señor Galvan was waiting for them. He hugged Rosa when she climbed out of the Jeep.

"I'm sorry I snapped at you over the phone, Rosa," he said. "I was almost crazy with worry. I even suspected Joe of conspiring with Frank to kidnap you. I don't know what I would have done if you hadn't called."

In the kitchen, Rosa washed her face while her uncle made hot tea.

"To tell you the truth," he said, "when you mentioned Ray Don Stanley and the guns, I was very surprised." Without looking up from the teakettle, he said, "If they are smuggling guns to the Montañeros, it's news to me."

"But we saw them," Rosa said.

"Yes, and I'll look into it as soon as this business with Rigo is over," Señor Galvan said.

Frank was impressed by Galvan's denial. If he's mixed up in this somehow, Frank thought, he's doing a pretty good acting job.

"But what about the money Ray Don Stanley is demanding from you?" Frank said.

"What money?" Galvan said. "What do you know about that?"

"It seems as if everybody knows," Frank said. "Even García."

Galvan's face seemed to fall. "Yes, he asked me about it earlier this evening," he admitted.

"So you don't know anything about Cisneros and his boat making a weapons run tonight?" Frank said. "Or about the explosion?"

Galvan looked shocked. "There was an explosion?" he said.

"Yes," Frank replied. "The police attacked the boat and it blew up."

Galvan cast his eyes down at the floor, twisting his hands in the pockets of his robe. "Not good," he muttered. "Not good at all."

"So you *do* know about the deliveries," Rosa said. "Why did you lie to me about it?"

He glanced at his niece. "Forgive me, Rosa. It's just that these dealings are highly sensitive. If my business partners got wind of it, they'd—" He broke off his sentence and gave her a long, hard look. "You understand why I do it, don't you? It is for your parents, my brother. But if anyone ever found out I was the one arming the Montañeros, I'd lose everything."

"But they took Rigo!" Rosa said. "You saw them yourself."

"I know," Galvan said. "Something has gone terribly wrong." He tugged at his lower lip, frowning. "I must make some telephone calls. You've got to excuse me. Please, you've both got to promise me complete secrecy. If word gets out, it would be a disaster."

Rosa said, *"Tío mío,* are you in danger?"

Galvan forced a smile. "Not as long as you keep what you've seen tonight a secret." He kissed her on the forehead. "Now go get some sleep."

Frank said good night to Rosa on the second-story landing. When he went into his bedroom, he was relieved to see Joe sound asleep in his bed. Frank considered waking his brother right then and there. He wanted to find out about Joe's trip on top of El Brujo's truck, but decided to get some sleep first.

Frank slept until two in the afternoon when Joe finally shook him awake. "Rise and shine, buddy," he said. "Luz has got lunch on the table."

Rosa was already eating her lunch when they went down and sat at the kitchen table. Between bites of his crabmeat sandwich, Frank managed to relate to Joe the events of the previous evening.

"All those guns being shipped to the Montañeros make me nervous," Joe said. "First the ones El Brujo delivered to Rancho Sonora, and how a boatload from Ray Don Stanley's warehouse."

"Except that the second load wound up at the bottom of the Gulf of Mexico," Frank said.

"Wait a minute," Rosa said. "Did you say Rancho Sonora?" Joe nodded. "That's where I was born."

"The Montañeros down there have not forgotten you," Joe said. "El Brujo told me they think of your parents as martyrs."

Rosa held herself very still, and Frank could tell she was struggling with the memory. "It was—terrible," she said, picking her words carefully. "And you can see why I am so fearful for my brother. Anytime you get between the Montañeros and the *policía*, it can get very dangerous."

"It's time we had another talk with El Brujo," Frank said. "He seems to know a lot more about the Montañeros than any of us."

"Let me talk to him alone," Joe said. "He's kind of strange, but I seem to get along pretty well with him. I don't want him to think we're accusing him of anything."

"Go for it," Frank said. "But before you do, let's see if Señor Galvan has turned up anything about last night's explosion."

The three teenagers went to the study where they found Lieutenant García and Señor Galvan. García didn't even greet them when he answered their knock on the study door. His face was an impassive mask. He nodded toward the desk, where a matador's pink stocking lay bunched in front of Señor Galvan, who stared at it in despair. It was stained with blood.

"It's Rigo's stocking," Rosa said.

Chapter

7

ROSA SNATCHED UP the bloodstained stocking. "What does this mean?" she cried.

"It just arrived by messenger," García said. "It came with a note. We are holding the messenger for questioning, but he knows nothing. The note says that your brother will be dead if the money is not delivered by tonight."

"They say if the money is not on the eight P.M. bus headed for Mexico City, then they will slit his throat," Galvan said.

"That gives us about four hours," Frank said, glancing at his watch. "What are your plans?"

"The money is to be placed in an unmarked brown suitcase," Galvan said. "They will pick it up in Mexico City at the main bus station. If the money isn't there, they will kill him. If it is, they will put him on the return bus to Matamoros. In no case are we to allow *policía* to interfere at either end, or we'll never see Rigo again."

"So you're just going to comply with the instructions?" Frank said. "What if they don't live up to their end of the bargain?"

"My men will be stationed at both ends of the bus trip," García said. "No uniforms, of course. That way, Señor Galvan will be safe when he makes the drop-off, and we'll be able to nab the Montañeros when they pick the money up in Mexico City."

"Sounds risky," Frank said.

"They could hijack the bus between here and there," Joe pointed out.

"Three *policía* will ride the bus—again, disguised," García answered.

"Sounds like you've got the situation covered," Frank said.

García could not hide the disdain in his voice. "Of course. What did you expect? Captain Martinez has arranged for our best undercover detectives to assist in the case. I'm sure we will capture the Montañeros."

"Lieutenant García," Joe said. "Why are you so sure it's the Montañeros who are behind all this?" García's eyes flickered back and forth between the two brothers.

"Of course it is," he said. "We all saw them at the bullfight."

Joe didn't reply, but Frank guessed he was thinking of El Brujo's denial that the Montañeros were behind the crime. Frank wanted to ask Señor Galvan why the Montañeros would snatch his nephew if he was supplying them with guns, but he remembered his sworn secrecy.

Rosa's uncle betrayed none of the confusion he must have been feeling. "I want you to come with me to the bus station, Rosa," he said. "With the *policía* around, it should be safer than here."

"But, Señor Galvan, we can take care of Rosa," Frank said. "We promised you."

A quick, hard glance from Galvan was enough to tell Frank that, after last night, he had lost his trust in their ability to perform that job.

"You and your brother will be comfortable here," Galvan said. "I don't want you leaving the premises."

Frank nodded and said, "We'll stay here," but he had a feeling Joe would try to convince him otherwise. Sure enough, as soon as they left the study and were out of earshot, Joe said, "I'm going to be on that bus."

"I'm not sure that's a good idea," Frank said. "Interfering with a police sting operation is likely to get us in big trouble."

"What kind of trouble could I be?" Joe said.

"I'll just be another American tourist with a camera."

Frank knew it was useless to try to talk Joe out of it. Besides, Joe was right. It was a big break in the case, and it would be a shame for them to sit on the sidelines.

"All right," Frank said, "but I'm going to follow the bus."

"Maybe you could borrow Rosa's Jeep," Joe said.

"No," Frank said, "I'll be too obvious in that red thing."

"How about Luz, the housekeeper?" Joe said. "She has a pickup truck parked out back. It would blend in with traffic. Maybe she'll let you borrow it for the night."

"Great idea," Frank said. "I'll go check on that and find out how to get to the bus station."

"Meanwhile, I'll go have my talk with El Brujo," Joe said.

Joe found the old matador in the barn, working by the light of the late afternoon sun at a tool bench beside a window. He was repairing a leather harness.

"I guess I learned a lesson during our little trip together," Joe said by way of greeting. "The only way to escape a bull is to keep your eye on its horns."

"A valuable lesson," the old man said, staring out the window.

"You taught that to Rigo, didn't you?" Joe said.

"Yes, I did," said the old man. "That's what makes him a better matador than others. You can't watch the eyes, not even for a second."

Changing the subject abruptly, Joe said, "You did a pretty good job of keeping our little meeting with Comandante Zeta a secret from Captain Martinez and Lieutenant García. But I think they know anyway." He explained how Frank had seen García at Ray Don Stanley's warehouse. "The lieutenant seemed pretty interested in where those weapons were going."

El Brujo's callused hands continued to work on the harness, even though his eyes never left the view out the window. "That fool," he said. "You didn't tell him what you saw at Rancho Sonora, did you?"

Joe shook his head. "I can't help thinking that García must have had something to do with the shrimp boat being intercepted."

"I see," El Brujo said, thinking for a moment. "But the land route is still safe."

"Are you planning another shipment?" Joe asked.

The hands stopped working on the leather, and El Brujo turned to Joe. "Stay out of it," he said flatly. "It is very dangerous. Things are heating up between the Montañeros and the *policía,* and both you and your brother will get hurt if you get involved."

"I think we already are involved," Joe said.

"That is your foolishness talking," said El Brujo. "You are taking your eyes off the horns. Be careful of your moves, my little friend. There isn't room for any mistakes."

"Don't talk in riddles," Joe said. "You know something about Rigo, don't you? Something you're not telling me."

The old man was silent.

"Are you a Montañero?" Joe asked.

"I was once accused of being a Montañero," replied El Brujo. "And I went to jail for being a Montañero. Does that make me one?" He sighed deeply and put the leather harness on the tool bench. "Now I am simply a teacher of bullfighters." He waved his hand. "Go, boy. Go and fight your bull. May the cleverest opponent win."

Joe started to leave. Before he did so, he heard the scratch and flare of a match. Glancing back, he saw El Brujo hold the flame to a candle. He said, "I will keep it burning until you return."

At 7:30 P.M. Lieutenant García, Rosa, and Señor Galvan left the ranch to deliver the money to the Matamoros bus station. Moments later Joe and Frank followed in the housekeeper's truck, a rusty old pickup with gardening tools rattling on a rack in the back.

"The ticket will cost you one hundred fifty pesos," Frank said as he shifted into high gear. "Do you have enough money?"

"Yes," Joe said.

"If anything goes wrong," Frank said, "hang your jacket out one of the windows on the bus. If worse comes to worst, I can pull up alongside and you can jump into the back."

The bus station was a large, modern one-story building on the edge of town. Joe spotted García behind the wheel of Galvan's car. "Don't get too close," he said.

Frank let the truck idle at the curb a block behind them. At seven-fifty Galvan got out of his car and walked quickly inside the station. He had the satchel in his hand. In his blue blazer and gray slacks, he looked like any prosperous Mexican businessman.

Moments later, he came out empty-handed, got into his car, and drove away.

"That's my cue," Joe said as soon as the coast was clear. "Wish me luck." He hopped out of the truck and hurried inside.

"I'll be right behind you," Frank said. "That's a promise."

"One way, señor?" asked the clerk at the ticket window.

"*Sí,*" Joe said.

A big blue-and-silver bus with Mexico

D.F.—meaning Mexico City—on the sign above the windshield was parked in one of the berths at the back of the station. Joe saw passengers hauling shopping bags and heavy suitcases, babies in their arms and small children in tow, through the narrow bus door. He wondered which ones were Martinez's undercover officers. Joe joined the line of passengers waiting to board.

Shortly after eight, the Mexico City–bound bus pulled out of the station and lumbered onto the highway access road. Frank followed about a hundred yards behind. As the bus sped up, heading out into traffic in the gathering dusk, Frank pressed the accelerator hard, hoping the housekeeper's truck had enough horsepower to keep up.

After twenty minutes on the highway, Frank was beginning to relax, anticipating an uneventful four-hour drive. There wasn't much traffic, and the heat had dissipated along with the light of day. Frank tuned the radio to an American rock-and-roll station.

Suddenly a large, black tow truck zoomed ahead of him in the passing lane. No headlights, no taillights. It must have been doing one hundred miles per hour. As it roared past Frank's open window, he could see that there was no license plate affixed to the rear bumper. Because the windows were tinted dark, he couldn't see who was driving or how many passengers were inside.

Frank floored it, attempting to catch up, but the housekeeper's truck was already straining at sixty miles per hour. He watched the tow truck pull in front of the bus, then veer hard into the bus's path. A shower of sparks and grinding metal marked the point of impact, and the bus started to spin out. The two vehicles, locked nose to nose, veered onto the shoulder of the freeway. Frank slammed on his brakes.

A cloud of dust enveloped the bus and tow truck as they fishtailed off the asphalt. As the dust cleared, Frank saw three armed men jump out of the tow truck. One sprinted toward the front of the bus, spraying machine-gun fire at the driver through the windshield. Another ran around to the side and managed to wrench the passenger door open and climb inside.

The third terrorist used his gun as a crowbar to leverage the luggage doors open. Boxes and baggage spilled onto the pavement, but the gunman knew what he was looking for. He snatched the leather satchel, ripped it open, and quickly checked its contents. Then he put the satchel back down on the pavement, ran over, and stepped up into the bus.

Frank jumped out onto the highway and shouted, "Stop!" The terrorist who had shot the bus driver squinted into the headlights of Frank's truck. Apparently he was temporarily blinded, because when he squeezed off a short burst of machine-gun fire, the bullets whizzed through the air over Frank's head. He dove for the dirt and rolled under the pickup.

In the silence that followed, Frank lifted his head. Were they gone? No, he heard another burst of gunfire that seemed to come from inside the bus. Frank heard a scream, then saw the two terrorists emerge from the bus.

"Viva la revolución!" one of them shouted, brandishing his rifle, as the other one grabbed the satchel of money and sprinted back to the tow truck.

The truck was already moving when the third masked gunman leaped onto the running board, opened the door, and swung inside.

Chapter

8

THE SHARP SMELL of burnt gunpowder greeted
Frank's nose when he scrambled up the steps
of the bus, his sneakers crunching on bits of
windshield glass. One glance at the bus driver
slumped over the steering wheel told Frank he
was dead. Sickened, he looked away, searching
the interior of the bus for Joe.

Headlights from the stalled traffic outside
the bus gave an eerie glow to the thin blue
smoke left behind by the rain of bullets. Some
of the passengers coughed; a baby started to
cry. Frank could hear someone in the back
moaning softly, but there were no screams, no
shouts of panic. He was surprised. It was a hor-
rible scene.

"Back here, Frank," Joe called.

Frank moved down the aisle and surveyed

the damage. There were three men wounded, two by bullets and the third with three slashes across his chest, probably from a big blade like a machete, Frank guessed. There were two horizontal cuts and a diagonal one, forming an unmistakable *Z* pattern.

Frank checked the slashed victim's pulse and felt a faint throb. "He's alive," he said.

The wounded man's eyelids fluttered, and he began to stir. "I am *policía*," he whispered. He took a breath and coughed weakly.

"Try to relax," Frank said, still assessing his wounds. Peeling back the man's shirt from his chest, Frank saw that, although they were bleeding heavily, the wounds were superficial. Whoever had attacked the man had only meant to mark him, not kill him.

"Comandante Zeta," said the undercover officer. "It was him."

"It's over," Frank said. "They're gone. You're going to be okay." A woman handed Frank a blanket, and he pressed it against the man's chest. Frank glanced down the aisle at Joe and said, "This guy is going to need medical attention right away."

"Same here," Joe said. "One of them caught it in the shoulder, the other in the leg."

"Get someone to put pressure on those wounds," Frank said. "I'll go for help."

Outside the bus, a small crowd of drivers, whose cars now blocked the highway in both directions, had gathered near the bus door, staring with horror at the driver's body. Frank emerged and asked, "Does anyone here speak English?"

A short, dark-skinned man in a tank top stepped forward. In his hand he held a cellular telephone. "I do," he said with a heavy accent. "I have called the *policía.*"

"Okay, tell these people to move their cars to the side of the road," Frank said. He heard the wail of sirens in the distance. "We're going to need to get ambulances through."

Frank went back inside the bus where Joe was supervising the care of the wounded men.

"Nobody else was hurt," Joe reported.

"They knew exactly who to go for," Frank said.

"Definitely a professional job," Joe said.

Frank told Joe the knifing victim had identified Comandante Zeta as his attacker. "You've seen Zeta and his guerrillas up close," Frank said. "Do you think it was them?"

Joe nodded. "Seems likely," he said. "I couldn't see any faces because they were wearing ski masks. But it could have been the same group from the chopper at the stadium."

"That means García is right," Frank said.

"And it makes El Brujo a liar," Joe said.

"The Montañeros probably used the same guns Señor Galvan has been shipping to them to kidnap Rigo and to launch this attack," Frank said, shaking his head in disgust.

"Galvan kept it a complete secret—even from García," Joe said. "So the Montañeros may not have known where their guns came from either."

"But I'm sure they're glad to have them," Frank said. "I guess Señor Galvan's plan really backfired on him."

They could see the flashing lights of the emergency vehicles approaching, trying to make their way through the snarled traffic.

"Let's get this over with, then go have another talk with El Brujo," Joe said.

Frank stepped out of the bus first and saw a police cruiser pull alongside. An unmarked car pulled up behind and Lieutenant García stepped out. When the young officer saw Frank and Joe standing by the bus, he pointed at them. "You two were told to stay out of this," he shouted. "I could have you arrested."

Galvan got out of the passenger seat of the unmarked car, and Rosa scrambled out from the rear door. "Frank! Joe!" she said. "Are you all right?"

"What are you doing here?" Galvan asked. "You're supposed to be at the ranch."

"There's been another attack," Frank explained. "It looks like it was the Montañeros again."

"What happened?" García asked.

"Go see for yourself," Joe said. "The bus driver's dead, and there are three wounded men on that bus. I think you'll recognize them."

"Just a minute," García said. "They didn't—" he stopped in midsentence and ran to jump on the bus to check on his wounded comrades.

"We were on our way back to the ranch after Uncle Ramon dropped off the money at the bus station," Rosa said, "when we got the call on Lieutenant García's radio." She looked fearfully at the bus. "Did you see Rigo with them?"

"No," Joe said. "But they marked the undercover police. And they took the money."

Galvan groaned and held his hand to his forehead. "This is worse than I thought."

"What do you mean?" Frank said.

"The money. It wasn't all there." Señor Galvan's normally calm face was now twisted in anguish. "I couldn't raise the entire amount so quickly. I couldn't even get half of it. So I filled the satchel with decks of playing cards and covered them over with a layer of real money."

"You *what?*" Rosa said.

"García said there would be no chance they would actually get the money when it arrived in Mexico City," Galvan said. "He assured me they would never find out it wasn't all there until it was too late."

"No wonder they attacked those undercover

cops," Frank said. "It was retaliation for your not living up to your end of the bargain."

"How could you do this?" Rosa cried. "You were risking my brother's life for a few million pesos."

"Rosa, please," said Galvan. "You must understand. We cannot simply give in to kidnappers and terrorists."

"Why? Because it turns out the terrorists are your friends the Montañeros?" Rosa asked.

García rejoined the group, saying, "It certainly looks as if the Montañeros have turned on you, Señor Galvan."

Frank could tell that García was shaken, for his face was pale and his mouth was set in a grim line. "It was Zeta, all right," he continued. "The signature is there."

Galvan's jaw muscles were clenched and he eyed García with a harsh glare. "I hold you responsible, Lieutenant García," he said. " 'Nothing can go wrong,' you told me. 'They'll never get their hands on that satchel.' Well, look what happened, Lieutenant, thanks to your advice."

"It wasn't supposed to happen this way," García said.

"What *was* supposed to happen, García?" Frank said. "Did you expect a bunch of terrorists to keep their word?"

"They were supposed to wait until Mexico

City," the officer said. "That was the plan. I guess I misjudged them."

"I'll say," Rosa said. "And probably ensured Rigo's death."

García's tone became officious. "I'm going to have to get statements from you two," he said to the Hardys. "I'll take the Galvans home myself. My colleagues will escort you to the station after the ambulances arrive. Then you can drive back to the ranch when you're finished."

"So what's your next move, Lieutenant?" Frank asked.

"What are you talking about?" García replied.

"How do you plan to find Rigo now?" Frank asked.

"The main concern right now is to get everyone out of sight and to safety," he said, glancing around in the darkness. "We're sitting ducks out here."

"They're gone," Frank said. "They're not going to launch another attack."

"They took off in that supercharged truck of theirs, and they're probably fifty miles away by now," Joe said, curious as to why García would be worried about another attack with all the police on the scene to protect them.

Frank and Joe were tied up for hours making statements at the Matamoros police station.

It was almost sunrise by the time they made it back to the ranch and parked the beat-up old pickup in the yard.

They were both exhausted, but Joe wasn't too tired to notice a glimmering light in the window of the barn. "That candle El Brujo lit for me is still burning," he said. "I wonder if the old guy is still awake."

"I would be if I were him," Frank said. "The police down at the station seemed pretty riled up about anyone who's suspected of being a Montañero. I heard one guy say they were going to do a big roundup of suspects today."

"Let's go check it out," Joe said.

The barn was silent and empty, except for the occasional rustling of horses. The predawn light filtered dimly through the window, so Joe blew out the nearly spent candle.

"I wonder where he sleeps," Joe said. At that moment they both heard the distant sound of breaking glass coming from outside the barn. They quickly found a door at the back of the barn. It led to a lower paddock. On the far side was a small adobe hut, where a light burned in the single window. Joe heard a snapping sound, followed by more glass breaking. With Frank, he crossed the paddock and peered into the open window.

They could see García, standing directly opposite the window, facing a smashed, glass-covered bookshelf. As they watched, García swept a whole row of books to the floor. "Where is it, old man?" he was saying. "Where are the delivery schedules? I know they're here somewhere."

Frank nudged Joe and pointed silently to the far left, making room for Joe to see farther into the hut. Joe saw El Brujo standing against the far wall, with his hands cuffed. There was a nasty-looking bruise on his forehead above his eye, but he watched quietly while García demolished his meager possessions.

The young officer crossed the room in a few short strides and confronted El Brujo face-to-face. "You may not be talking now, but when I get you down to the station, you'll loosen your lips. That's a promise. Until then," he said, curling his hand into a fist and drawing it back to strike the elderly matador, "I want you to remember this as a taste of what's to come."

"No," Joe shouted impulsively, his voice carrying loud through the open window. The lieutenant drew his pistol and whirled in one smooth motion. He took aim at the window and started to squeeze the trigger.

Chapter

9

"DON'T SHOOT," Joe said through the window. "It's us, Frank and Joe Hardy."

García crossed the room and opened the door, keeping his pistol leveled as his eyes focused on Frank and Joe.

García was about to say something, but Joe beat him to the punch. "What are you doing to the old man?" he said.

"Police business," he replied. "I already told you to stay out of it."

"Seems like we interfered at just the right time," Frank said. "You were about to strike a handcuffed man. Is that part of your job description?"

"He is under arrest for conspiring with the Montañeros," García said, lowering his gun. "I can do as I like with him."

"Is there any connection with Rigo's kidnapping?" Joe said.

García's answer was clipped. "I have already warned you too many times. If you do not stop interfering in this case, I'll be forced to arrest you for obstruction of justice."

Peering in through the door, Joe briefly locked eyes with El Brujo, who gave a nod as if to say he could take care of himself. Joe said, "Okay, okay, we're leaving." He and Frank turned and headed back across the paddock toward the barn. When they reached it, Joe glanced back at El Brujo's hut and saw García watching them from the doorway.

"I don't see what else we can do right now," Frank said, "without getting ourselves arrested."

"García thinks the police can torture some information out of the old man," Joe said. "There's no way they're going to get anything out of him that way. Even if he does know something about where they're holding Rigo."

"But he admitted being a Montañero, didn't he?" Frank said. "So he must know something about it. If only we could talk to him, we might be able to coax something out of him."

They looked up at the house, which was now bathed pink in the light from the rising sun.

"Let's go talk to Rosa," Joe said. "She might have some ideas about how to get in touch with him once he's at the jailhouse."

"It's worth a try," Frank said.

It was just before six o'clock and Rosa was not happy at being woken up. When Frank made it clear that El Brujo was being arrested, though, she sat up in bed and rubbed her eyes.

"Why would they take him?" she said.

"I guess because he knows where to deliver weapons to Zeta," Frank replied. "They must figure that if they can find Zeta and the Montañeros, then they'll find Rigo."

"There they go," Joe said, peering out the second-story window.

Rosa climbed out of bed and joined Joe at the bedroom window. García shoved El Brujo, still handcuffed, into a police cruiser, then stood and watched as the car pulled away. Seconds later he went back into the house through the kitchen door.

"I'm going to wake my uncle," Rosa said. "Maybe he can do something."

"We'll wait in our room," Frank said.

Joe threw himself on his bed and let out a big yawn. All these late nights were catching up to him. "Do you still think Zeta is the one holding Rigo?" he wondered.

Frank sat in an armchair at the foot of Joe's bed. "It just doesn't make sense," Frank said, yawning. "I mean, you said Zeta and his gang consider Rigo and Rosa's parents heroes."

"If it wasn't Zeta's gang, then who else could have kidnapped him?" Joe murmured.

Frank didn't answer. He was already sound asleep. Joe promised himself just a short catnap, but before long he, too, had fallen into a deep sleep.

Two hours later Joe woke up to a jangling in his ear. Rosa stood over him, holding the keys to her Jeep.

"Rise and shine," she said. "My uncle gave me permission to go see El Brujo in jail. Under the condition, of course, that you and your brother go with me. I guess you earned back some of his trust by the way you handled yourselves during the bus attack."

The Matamoros jail was an ugly stone hulk of a building just off the downtown plaza. Police guards with machine guns stood at the massive prison doors, which were open to the street and big enough to drive a truck through. With impassive eyes, the guards watched Rosa, Frank, and Joe walk through the entrance and up to another officer in a glass booth just inside the courtyard.

"We are here to see the prisoner known as El Brujo," Rosa explained.

The guard glanced suspiciously at her. Seeing Rosa smile sweetly, he shoved a clipboard through a slot in the glass. "Sign here and put on these badges," he said. "I'll call an escort for you."

"Not exactly a cheerful place," Joe whispered to Frank while another guard led them into the damp cinder-block building. They passed through two iron doors and two more sets of guards before reaching the corridor of holding cells. El Brujo's cell was at the end of a long, narrow hallway. Its unpainted walls sweated foul-smelling beads of water in the dank air, and its high windows allowed almost no daylight to filter in through the bars.

The guard leading them halted at the opposite end of the hallway. El Brujo already had a visitor. "One at a time," he said gruffly. "You'll have to wait your turn."

Joe peered past the guard and saw a man in an expensive-looking blue suit talking to the old matador through the bars. "Who is that?" he asked.

"His lawyer," replied the guard.

Joe turned to look at Rosa. "He has a lawyer?"

"Not that I know of," Rosa said. "Maybe my uncle called one of his lawyers to look out for him."

Joe scrutinized the man's profile. Even in the dim light, he could see a handlebar mustache. When the distinguished-looking man turned his head, spotting Joe, he cut his conversation with El Brujo short. With his head down, he hurried toward them. "Excuse me, *por favor,*" he said as he passed them in the narrow corridor.

Joe reached out, grabbed his shoulder, and spun him around for a closer look. It was Comandante Zeta. Joe stood still in shock. The elusive young Montañero chief took the opportunity to duck out from under Joe's hand and hurry down the hall toward the exit.

"Who was that?" Frank said.

"Zeta," Joe said.

Joe turned to follow Zeta, who was already halfway down the hall. He had gone only two steps when an explosion rocked the building, throwing him forward onto his hands and knees. The corridor quickly filled with dust and smoke. The deafening blast produced a loud ringing in Joe's eardrums and he choked on the thick air.

Frank was knocked up against the cinderblock wall and a biting pain shot through his shoulder. At first he thought he might have broken his collarbone.

"Are you all right?" Rosa asked. She had been thrown up against Frank, whose body cushioned her impact. Frank moved his shoulder a little. It still hurt badly, but he could tell it wasn't broken.

"Where's Joe?" he gasped.

Rosa peered into the thick, swirling dust that seemed to originate from El Brujo's cell. "I don't see him," she replied. Somewhere back by the guard's station an emergency siren started to wail.

"Back here," Joe said, emerging from El Brujo's cell. His face and clothes were smudged with flash burns, but he was otherwise unharmed. "Are you guys okay?"

"Barely," Frank said, wincing as he moved his shoulder.

"Let's move," Joe said anxiously. "El Brujo's gone. Zeta must have brought in a load of dynamite. It blew a big hole in the outside cell wall."

Sunlight streamed in through the jagged hole in the wall of El Brujo's cell, providing a clear escape route through a paved courtyard that looked like an outdoor exercise area for prisoners. There was no sign of El Brujo or anyone else.

Stepping gingerly over the rubble, Joe led Frank and Rosa through the hole. He spotted a metal door marked *Policía Solamente* and headed toward it. The courtyard was surrounded by four high walls topped with razor wire. Joe figured the door had to be the only means of escape.

A pair of guards burst through the door and rushed right past them, heading toward the prison cells. Joe caught the door before it slammed shut, and they went inside where there was a hallway lined with administrative offices.

"Quick, over there," Rosa said, pointing to an exit sign over a second metal door at the end of the hallway. The door led to a fire escape. They took it down to the street where they could see the large prison doors closing. From inside the jail, they could hear shouting over the sound of alarms.

Breathless, the three paused for a moment on the sidewalk. One of the guards shouted something in Spanish to his partner and pointed across the street to a small open-air market. There were several fruit and vegetable stands with brightly colored awnings occupying an open lot. Joe peered in that direction and spotted El Brujo limping quickly along the sidewalk.

At the same time a battered Volkswagen with dust-covered windows and rusted-out fenders came rattling down the street toward them. It swerved over to the curb and the passenger door opened. Joe caught a glimpse of Zeta behind the wheel as El Brujo dove into the still-rolling vehicle and slammed the door behind him. The vehicle sped up, emitting a cloud of bluish gray exhaust.

With a sinking feeling in the pit of his stomach, Joe watched one of the guards aim his machine gun at the car. A rattle of bullets ripped through the air and a line of jagged holes stitched its way down one side of the rusty little car.

The car swerved, hopped the curb, and crashed into one of the vegetable stands, sending food flying. The vendor dove out of the way, just in time to avoid being crushed by the car's round front fender.

Amazingly, Zeta was able to control the car as it skidded through the empty lot, with fruit and vegetables falling away from its roof. It bounced over the curb again and headed off down a side street as several more bursts from the guard's machine guns missed their mark.

Frank was already sprinting toward the Jeep, with Rosa and Joe close behind him, when he heard another shout from one of the guards. He picked up speed, crouching low and zigzagging. "Hurry up," he shouted over his shoulder, expecting to be riddled with bullets any second.

They had only a few more yards to go before they reached the shelter of the Jeep. But they were running unprotected, and for all the prison guards knew, they were the ones who had organized El Brujo's jailbreak.

Chapter

10

As JOE SPRINTED toward the Jeep, following Frank and Rosa, he glanced over his shoulder. The guards were shouting at their comrades inside the prison doors, which had begun to open.

When they reached the Jeep, Rosa tossed the keys to Frank and said, "You drive. Just get us out of here fast."

Frank fired up the vehicle and made a U-turn in the street, leaning into the corner as he shot up a parallel side street, away from the guards and their machine guns.

"Cut over to the next street," Joe said from the backseat. "I think that's where Zeta went. Maybe we can pick up his trail."

As precious moments passed, the three searched the side streets for Zeta's car, but they saw no sign of it.

"I guess we lost them," Frank said.

"Where would they go?" Joe said.

"No telling," Rosa said. "The Montañeros are known to come and go like the wind."

"Any suggestions?" Frank asked.

"I wonder if—" Rosa said, then shook her head, saying, "Never mind, it's a silly idea."

"At this point, anything's a good idea," Frank said.

"I was just thinking of Luz, our housekeeper," Rosa said. "She lives around here. She used to bring me to her home. She lives with twelve of her relatives. Of course, they are very poor—she is the only one with a job—and their house is very small, but they have treated me very kindly."

"Would they know anything about El Brujo?" Frank asked.

"That's what I was thinking," Rosa said. "Even though he hasn't fought for years, the people still remember him as the greatest matador in history. Especially among the poor people of Mexico, he is still very popular. He would find a lot of support in Luz's neighborhood."

"Zeta and El Brujo have got to ditch that car pretty soon," Joe said. "I doubt they'll get very far if they don't. Let's go ask around Luz's neighborhood. Maybe somebody there will have seen them."

Rosa directed them to one of the poorest

sections of Matamoros. The dwellings were built of anything the people could find—cast-off pieces of lumber, strips of tin, plastic sheets, cement blocks. The road was rutted dirt, packed hard and dry. It looked like a junkyard, Frank thought, as they parked in front of a tiny shack made of corrugated tin. Still, here and there he could see signs of civic pride. The dirt yards were neatly swept, and some of the shacks even had hand-painted numbers out front.

Rosa disappeared into the shack, while Frank and Joe stayed in the Jeep. Watching a hen scratch in the dirt in the road, Frank said, "That was a pretty bold move on Zeta's part. I'm impressed."

Joe had to agree. It took a lot of guts to go into such a well-fortified prison and blast your way out like that. "You'd think he would have used the same truck he used last night, when he ambushed the bus," Joe said. "I mean, that little tin heap he's driving now looks like it would fall apart if you got it going over forty miles per hour."

"Right," Frank said. "And come to think of it, where did he get that helicopter to kidnap Rigo in the first place?"

"Good question," Joe said. He sat up in his seat and looked around. "Frank, did you see that woman down the street?"

"Yes," Frank said. "She just went into the shack next door."

"That's the third time she's done that," Joe said.

At that moment Rosa appeared with another woman, who glanced briefly at the boys in the Jeep, then hurried next door. Rosa approached the Jeep and said, "That was Luz's sister. I explained what happened, and she said she'd ask around. She'll be back in a little while."

"It looks like word is going around the neighborhood pretty fast," Frank said.

Feeling his stomach rumble, Joe spoke up from the backseat. "Is there anyplace around here where we can get a taco or something? I'm starved."

"I think I smell something cooking out back," Rosa said. "I can ask if they have enough to spare."

"I don't know about that," Frank said. "These people seem awfully poor. I wouldn't want to be taking the only food they have to eat."

"Nonsense," Rosa said. "Our poor people are generous, and they would never refuse a meal to a friend in need. I'll be right back."

Rosa went around the back of the shack, and moments later an old woman with a withered face and sunken eyes emerged. She motioned for the two brothers to follow her to the backyard of the tiny, ramshackle house. There was an open fire with a blackened pot on it. Inside the pot, there was a thick soup of red beans bubbling away. Another steaming pot held white rice.

The old woman seated the Hardys at a makeshift table where Rosa waited. She served them hearty helpings of the rice with the bean soup ladled on top. She added some fried bananas on the side of each plate.

Several people were seated on wooden crates and chairs that were arranged underneath the single tree in the yard. A couple of children played an elaborate game with sticks in the dust, glancing curiously at the visitors and whispering shyly from time to time.

Frank and Joe gratefully gobbled up their plates of rice and beans. The food was simple and delicious. Rosa was just beginning to tell them about Luz's family when she was interrupted by the sister returning from next door. She spoke rapidly in Spanish, while Rosa translated.

"She's saying that the people in the neighborhood are all talking about the jailbreak," she said. "They are saying El Brujo has his old bullfighting magic back."

"Do they know where he is?" Rosa asked.

"Maybe," Rosa said. "She says that if anyone would know, it would be"—she paused, listening carefully—"it would be at the house of a Señor Cifuentes. He is the unofficial mayor of the neighborhood. It's not far from here."

"Let's go," Joe said. "The longer we wait, the better the chance they'll disappear into the countryside. Then we'll never find them."

After thanking Luz's sister, the three climbed back into the Jeep and drove a short distance to another part of the neighborhood. This dwelling had a fruit stand out in front, a table loaded with bananas, guavas, pineapples, and sugarcane. A canvas roof held up with rough-cut timber kept the sun off the fruit.

Rosa knocked at the door behind the fruit stand, with Frank standing right beside her. "Come in," said a voice from inside. The door opened to reveal a small, dimly lit room. Frank could see well enough to make out the face of Comandante Zeta, sitting casually on a sagging couch. He could also see the outline of a shotgun, aimed directly at his chest.

"*Hola, muchachos,*" the young man said. He glanced past Frank to his brother. "Señor Joe, we meet again, *sí?*" He was still wearing his lawyer's blue suit, white shirt, and striped tie, but they were wrinkled and smudged now. His face, Joe noticed, was as sharp and cunning as he remembered from their first meeting at Rancho Sonora.

"Where is El Brujo?" Joe asked.

"Here," Zeta answered politely, waving his

gun. Joe came farther into the little room and saw El Brujo on a thin pallet on the floor. His face was swollen, especially around his eye, and he held his left hand gingerly, where a blood-soaked bandage had been hastily tied.

Rosa ran to his side and touched his forehead. "Are you all right?" she said.

Joe joined Rosa and saw him nod weakly. "I guess you still know how to avoid the horns of a bull," Joe said.

The man's leather face wrinkled into a smile, but Joe could tell it gave him pain. Turning to Zeta, Joe said, "That was a pretty dramatic exit this afternoon. Do you do that for all of your Montañeros?"

"Only when one of them is unjustly arrested," Zeta replied.

"Comrades?" Frank said, looking at El Brujo. "He seems like more than just a friend."

"Correct," Zeta said. "He has been delivering supplies to us. He is our link to our benefactor."

"You mean my uncle?" Rosa said.

"I know better than to question who it is," Zeta replied. "We are merely grateful for whatever help we are given. If it is your uncle who has been supplying us, then God bless him."

"You accept my uncle's generosity in the name of my parents," Rosa said, "then you turn around and kidnap my brother. I demand that you tell me where he is."

"We don't have him," Zeta said.

"But we saw you," Joe said. "First at the bullfighting ring, then at the bus."

"That was not me, nor was it the Montañeros," Zeta said. "Those are impostors posing as Montañeros. They're attempting to discredit our revolution."

"You mean, you didn't carve up that guy on the bus?" Joe said.

Zeta frowned. "Of course not. I am insulted you would suspect me of endangering innocent people like that. My complaints are with the *policía* and with the government, not the people of Mexico. I wage war, but I do not do it where innocent lives will be lost."

"So who would it be?" Frank asked.

"I don't know," Zeta replied, "but I have my suspicions. It must be someone working for the *policía*. Who else would want to discredit our cause? They want the Mexican people to believe the Montañeros are indiscriminate killers, to turn the tide of popular sentiment against us. So they staged the kidnapping, but what nobody seemed to realize was that the man these so-called Montañeros targeted was actually supplying us with the few weapons we have. Even the massacre on the bus was staged to make the Montañeros look bad. That way, the *policía* can arrest El Brujo, treat him with disrespect, and wage war against us with the support of the Mexican people."

"Talk about a negative public relations campaign . . ." Joe said with a whistle.

"Correct," Zeta said. "And now our weapon supply is in danger. Without it, our cause may be crushed. Believe me," he said to Rosa, "we are desperately trying to find your brother. But we must also defend ourselves."

El Brujo looked up at Rosa from his mat on the floor. "I hope you didn't believe Ruperto García when he accused me of being behind Rigo's kidnapping."

"I didn't want to believe it," she said, her voice trembling. "But with my own eyes I saw what I thought were Montañeros take my brother." She wiped her eyes hastily. "I am glad to know the truth now."

El Brujo pulled himself up on his elbows, wincing, and spoke to Zeta. "They should not get involved. It is too dangerous, and if Rosa were to meet the same fate as her brother, I would not be able to live with myself."

"But they could be useful to us now," Zeta argued. "We've got to reestablish contact with Galvan to arrange for tomorrow morning's shipment. They have free access to him, even under the noses of the *policía.*"

"No," Brujo said. "I will drive the truck, as always. By tonight I will be as good as new. I'll sneak back to the ranch, get the truck, and drive it down to Rancho Sonora, just as we originally planned."

"It's too risky," Zeta said. "If Galvan pays Ray Don Stanley, and if Stanley makes the delivery without the *policía* intercepting it, as they did last time, then you'll still be a fugitive from justice. You'll never get through it alive."

"I could talk to my uncle," Rosa said. "Once he learns that you are not the ones holding Rigo, you'll have his full support again."

"Little Rosa," El Brujo said. "I do not want you to get hurt."

"I won't," she said. "But you must allow me to help, for the sake of Rigo."

"Who will make the delivery then?" Zeta said.

"Maybe Ray Don Stanley could arrange for one of his employees to deliver it," Frank suggested.

"I'll bet he has plenty of border guards on his payroll," Joe said. "Once they're inside Mexico, they could drop off the shipment just about anywhere."

Frank could tell the idea appealed to Zeta, for he quickly scribbled some instructions on a piece of paper. "If they leave the weapons here," he said, handing the paper to Rosa, "we will pick them up by eleven A.M. tomorrow." As she accepted the piece of paper, he gripped her hand tightly. "Consider this a promise: I will find out who is holding your brother."

"I hope so," she replied. She kneeled beside El Brujo, taking his hand in hers. "I must go now." She bent to kiss his forehead above his bruised eye. "Heal yourself, Magician," she said. "Your people need you."

As they drove back to the ranch, they went over their plan to work with their new ally, Comandante Zeta, to find Rigo. The Hardys weren't too pleased about getting involved with the weapons shipment from Ray Don Stanley to the Montañeros. But Rosa pointed out that it was probably the only way they could guarantee Zeta would help them find Rigo.

"Stanley can't be trusted as far as you can throw him," Joe said. "What's to stop him from taking Galvan's money, then letting the police know about the delivery so they can skim some off the top, just like he did with the shrimp boat?"

Frank checked his watch. "It's three o'clock now. We'll get back to the ranch in a few minutes. That leaves a couple of hours for Señor Galvan to set up the deal. Then you and I could go to Stanley's warehouse, stake it out, and step in if anything goes wrong."

"But what if the *policía* do stage a confrontation?" Rosa said. "If it's anything like last time, you won't be able to do anything about it."

Both brothers knew she was right, and they fell silent, realizing that this time they might have gotten themselves in over their heads.

When they pulled into the driveway at the ranch, Lieutenant García's car was not in its usual spot. The house was quiet. Rosa went directly to the study and opened the door, expecting to see her uncle sitting behind his desk.

At first Frank thought he wasn't there. Then he heard Rosa let out a low gasp. She pointed to the floor on the far side of the desk, where a hand was just visible. Rushing around the desk, Rosa found her uncle lying flat on his back, a small puddle of blood under his head.

Chapter

11

Rosa CRADLED HER uncle's head in her hands. Frank quickly stooped beside him and found a pulse. "He's only unconscious," he said. Gently removing Rosa's hands from her uncle's head, he checked his air passage and determined that his breathing was clear.

"Will he be all right?" Rosa asked.

"We shouldn't move him," Joe said.

"Do you have any smelling salts?" Frank asked.

Rosa nodded and fetched a bottle. Frank waved them under Señor Galvan's nostrils. Galvan's head jerked as he whiffed the aroma. Then he uttered a low moan.

"Uncle Ramon," Rosa said. "It's me."

Señor Galvan's eyes opened, and he squinted up at his niece. "Rosa," he whispered.

"Don't move," Frank said. "You have a head injury."

Galvan turned his head slightly, grimacing with pain, but he managed to sit up. "I don't think it's too bad."

Frank examined the wound. "Looks like you were pistol-whipped," he said. "Who did this?"

"Ruperto García," Señor Galvan said. "We were having an argument."

"About what?" Joe asked.

"When he heard about El Brujo's escape from jail, he went crazy," Señor Galvan said. "He—he just went crazy. I guess he was upset over losing his most valuable suspect."

"We saw El Brujo, Uncle Ramon," Rosa said. "After he escaped from jail."

"You what?" said Señor Galvan, surprised. "Did you talk to him? Does he know anything about Rigo?"

"Not exactly," she answered, "but he did say that the Montañeros are definitely not responsible for the kidnapping."

If Señor Galvan was surprised before, he was astonished now. "You mean, they didn't—"

"No," she answered. "He says it's a group of terrorists posing as Montañeros."

"They may have wanted to get the ransom money and discredit the Montañeros at the same time by blaming it on them," Frank added.

"What they didn't count on was that you were secretly supplying the Montañeros with weapons," Joe said.

"But who could it be?" asked Señor Galvan.

"Zeta promised he would try to find out," Rosa said. "But he needs supplies desperately." She briefly explained how the weapons delivery from Ray Don Stanley had to be completed, but without El Brujo serving as the delivery man.

"That scheduled delivery tomorrow morning," Galvan said, "is what García and I argued about. He wanted to know when it was, but I wouldn't tell him. He threatened me. I threatened him. I suppose I provoked him, then finally he attacked me."

"He may have searched the office after he knocked you out," Joe said, "and found out about it."

"He couldn't have," Galvan said. "I keep no records of the transactions here."

Rosa held up the scrap of paper Zeta had given her. "And even if you did, García couldn't have found out about this delivery—unless he's clairvoyant."

"I could arrange with Ray Don to have his men drive the shipment anywhere in Mexico," Galvan said. "Usually they drop it off here, and El Brujo takes it to Rancho Sonora along with the bull deliveries, but we could change the instructions now."

"I think you'd better do that," Frank said. He went on to explain their plan to shadow the shipment. Galvan tried to dissuade them, but he gave in when they convinced him it was their best chance of finding Rigo. If the shipments continued to go through, Comandante Zeta would guarantee that they would have a whole army of Montañeros looking for the young bullfighter.

Frank and Joe hid the Jeep in one of the abandoned storage sheds across the street from Ray Don Stanley's warehouse. Then they found a safe lookout spot behind a couple of large Dumpsters. It was past midnight, but the heat of the day clung to the waterfront like a hot, wet blanket. The air was still, and Frank could feel rivulets of sweat trickling down his back under his shirt.

Joe gazed over at the rusty metal warehouse, which was lit by floodlights. "This is where the shrimp boats load their cargo?" he asked.

"That's right," Frank said. "There's a dock in back that sticks out into the bay."

They staked out the warehouse all night, taking turns resting and watching. As dawn broke, the shrimp boats headed out into the Gulf for their daily catch, occasionally blasting their horns, which echoed across the quiet town. Soon Frank and Joe saw a big semitractor-trailer rig pull up to the warehouse, its running lights shining brightly in the predawn gloom.

There was a larger-than-life likeness of Ray Don Stanley's smiling face painted on the side of the trailer. It showed him wearing a big western hat and string tie. He was cradling a submachine gun in his arms.

Two workers heaved the warehouse doors open and guided the tractor-trailer as it backed up to the loading dock. A forklift loaded with a stack of crates for the semitrailer emerged from the warehouse. The forklift made seven or eight more trips. When the semi was loaded, the trailer doors were locked, and the driver climbed back into the cab. He started the powerful engine, and the truck began pulling away from the warehouse.

"Let's follow him," Joe said.

"No, let's wait," Frank said. "I don't think they'd be running guns into Mexico with a huge picture of Ray Don Stanley on the side of the trailer."

"I guess you're right," Joe said.

Half an hour later, just as Joe was starting to feel drowsy again, a battered old panel truck pulled up in front of the warehouse. This truck had an entirely different sign painted on its side: It was a dead cockroach lying on its back, with its antennae limp and its skinny legs pointed straight up in the air. *No mas cucara-chas!* the sign said. "No more cockroaches!"

"An exterminator," Joe said. "Do you think they use machine guns to get rid of roaches around here?"

As the panel truck pulled into the loading dock, the Hardys saw Ray Don Stanley himself come out to greet it. He shook hands with the driver, a dark-haired young man wearing what appeared to be the uniform of the exterminating company.

Ray Don turned toward the front door and yelled for the forklift operator. Moments later he appeared driving a large crate.

"That's the same kind of crate Rosa and I saw on that shrimp boat that blew up," Frank said.

The warehouse workers carefully wedged three of the crates into the panel truck. By then it was riding low to the ground.

"Let's go," Frank said, heading back toward the spot where the Jeep was hidden. Joe followed and they took off, giving the exterminator's truck a one-block head start, then fell in behind it. The heavily loaded truck made its way along back streets to the international bridge across the Rio Grande.

By now the sun was up, and several vehicles waited to cross the border into Mexico. The Hardys found themselves stuck behind a truck loaded with a mountain of tomatoes. Joe leaned out the window to keep the exterminator's van in sight. He saw it ahead of them. The customs officer, wearing a police uniform, waved it through the barrier without glancing inside.

"Ray Don must have paid good money for that," Joe said.

"He's probably got a lot of the border guards and customs officials on his payroll," Frank said.

The Hardys weren't as lucky as Stanley's exterminator, however. The officer stopped them and said to Frank, "Your driver's license, señor."

Frank handed the officer his driver's license. Joe tried to keep his eyes on the panel truck as it headed into downtown Matamoros.

"This is your Jeep, Señor Hardy?" the officer asked.

"Well, no," Frank said. "It belongs to a friend. Excuse me, sir, but we're in a bit of a hurry."

"I'm sure you are, young man," the officer said with a polite nod and a smile. "Everybody is, but we have to be on the lookout for stolen vehicles." The officer went back inside the booth and got on the phone. After what seemed like an interminable wait, the officer returned and handed Frank's license back to him. "Have a nice visit," he said, waving the Jeep forward.

Frank gunned the motor, and Rosa's Jeep shot across the bridge to the Mexican side. Joe frantically searched the street ahead of them. Then he slapped his palm against the dashboard. "We lost him," he said. He peered up and down every side street as they drove into downtown Matamoros.

"No, we didn't," Frank said. "You can always count on Matamoros traffic." The truck was stopped at a traffic light a block ahead of the Hardys.

The Hardys kept the van in sight as it made its way through town. It wasn't long before they were back on the familiar highway going south in the direction of Rancho del Mar. They were the only car on the road behind the exterminator's van, so Frank had to hang well back. Although he could see the van ahead on the straight stretches of the country road, it frequently disappeared behind curves.

Rounding one curve, they were surprised to see the van they were following stopped dead in the middle of the road. It was sideways as if it had fishtailed to a stop. On the other side of it was a police car, with the red lights on its roof revolving. The driver was just climbing out of the van.

Frank hit the brakes, and the Jeep slowed. He started to turn the wheel. They were about fifty yards from the two vehicles. Joe couldn't believe his eyes when he recognized the police officer who had stopped the van. It was Ruperto García.

The muscular officer was standing in the middle of the road, holding a submachine gun pointed at the driver of the exterminator's van. When the Jeep came into view, García seemed puzzled or surprised for an instant. Then he seemed to recognize Rosa's Jeep and its driver. He swung the gun around to point at them.

Frank wheeled the Jeep around in a tight U-turn. As he accelerated in the opposite direction, heading back toward Matamoros, Joe turned to look back through the rear window. He saw García taking aim and squeezing the trigger. There were several rapid yellow flashes from the muzzle of the gun. A fraction of a second later the Jeep's rear window shattered, spraying glass fragments.

Joe ducked as a bullet ricocheted off the rim of the front windshield and hit where his head had been a moment before. To get out of the line of fire, Frank yanked the steering wheel hard to the right, running the Jeep off the asphalt and onto the sandy shoulder. It skidded over several bumps, digging its right wheels into the soft dirt and tilting sharply as if it were about to roll over. Frank struggled for control.

Chapter

12

THE JEEP'S REAR END was fishtailing wildly. Frank stayed with it, though, coolly accelerating until the spinning wheels bit into the solid asphalt again and the Jeep leaped forward. Once he regained control, he zigzagged away, pressing his foot hard on the gas.

As Frank shifted into third gear, he heard Joe saying, "We've got to go back, that was Lieutenant García!"

Frank wasn't sure if he'd heard Joe right, but he did hear another staccato burst from the submachine gun. "No way," he said. "That guy is shooting to kill."

The Jeep was going close to seventy miles per hour as two more quick bursts from García's submachine gun missed their mark. They rounded the curve and slowed down to cruising speed.

"He must have found out about the delivery," Joe said. "The question is how."

"Could be Ray Don Stanley," Frank said. "I wouldn't be surprised if that slime is playing both ends of the game, taking money from Galvan, and then turning around and feeding information to García."

"Is there any chance García could be part of a legitimate police investigation?" Joe said.

"I doubt it," Frank said. "The minute he saw it was us, he opened fire. I'm beginning to think that our friend Lieutenant García is one corrupt cop. You heard what Rosa's uncle said about him—he just about went crazy on him. Now this."

"Let's give Captain Martinez a call," Joe said, reaching for Rosa's car phone. "Maybe he knows what García is up to." Joe dug the police chief's card out of his pocket and dialed his private number. Captain Martinez answered on the first ring. He told Joe he had no idea where García was.

"He didn't check in this morning," Martinez said. "He's supposed to be protecting Señor Galvan at his ranch, but I checked there and they told me he didn't show up for work today."

"We've got some news for you, Captain Martinez," Joe said. "We just saw Ruperto out on the highway on the way to Señor Galvan's ranch. He intercepted a gun smuggler we were following. When we pulled up, he started blasting away and shot out the back window of Rosa's Jeep."

"He's certainly not acting under my orders," Captain Martinez said in a voice that sounded thin and tense. "I'll send some men out there to check this out. Meanwhile, I want you two to come down to the station right away."

Glancing back at the empty highway behind them through the shattered rear window, Joe said, "Yes, sir. I don't think we could make it to the ranch at this point, anyway, not without an armored vehicle."

"I hope whoever he sends for García has plenty of backup," Joe said after he hung up. "I'd guess García is going to put up a good fight."

"I'm afraid our little surprise meeting has interrupted García's ambush," Frank said. "I doubt he's hanging around waiting for us to come back."

"If he's going to bolt," Joe said, "shouldn't we go back and try to follow him?"

Frank looked up ahead and saw two police cars heading their way, sirens blaring and lights flashing. "Let's just let them do their jobs and go see Captain Martinez," Frank said. "I don't know about you, Joe, but I think we've dodged enough bullets—at least for this morning."

*   *   *

The police station was next door to the prison where Comandante Zeta had staged El Brujo's daring jailbreak. The Hardys were directed to Captain Martinez's office where he sat behind his desk talking on the telephone. He beckoned them to come in and take a seat as he hung up.

"I don't have any reports on Lieutenant García yet," he said, "but I should get something soon."

Frank took a chair near the desk, while Joe remained standing. The captain continued, "You boys seem to handle yourselves pretty well in some tough situations, which is why I don't mind sharing some confidential information with you. Lieutenant García has been acting very strange lately. The way he handled El Brujo's arrest and the escape afterward was totally unprofessional. I think the pressure of his job has gotten to him. Still, I must say I was surprised at what you told me."

"That van was full of smuggled guns," Joe said, "probably meant for the Montañeros, so it would make sense for García to seize the load."

"As soon as he started shooting at us, though," Frank said, "we knew that it wasn't official police business. Of course, he knows we're on to him now."

The captain's intercom buzzed. "Martinez," he said, snatching up the receiver and pressing it to his ear. He listened for several moments, nodding, then he said something decisively and hung up. Frank thought the captain's face registered a combination of surprise and anger.

"That was one of the officers on the scene," he said. "Our men have found the truck and the driver. He is dead. He was an American who worked for Ray Don Stanley."

"Where's García?" Frank asked.

"We don't know," Martinez said. "The truck was only partly loaded with weapons. They suspect the rest had already been unloaded into García's vehicle."

"So you think García was trying to hijack the shipment?" Joe asked.

"Exactly," Martinez said quietly. "It looks as if Ruperto García has betrayed my trust and his obligation to the citizens of Matamoros. We must pursue him and arrest him immediately."

"There's one other person we think you should go after, sir," Frank said. "Ray Don Stanley. He's been shipping weapons to the Montañeros."

Martinez listened without expression to this news. Then he said, "We've known about Stanley for a long time, but we can't touch him as long as he's on the U.S. side of the border. It would help if we could find out where the money is coming from."

"I think we can help you with that, too, Captain," Joe said. "It's Señor Galvan. He's been bankrolling the shipments to the Montañeros."

"This is a very serious accusation," Martinez said. "Are you sure about it?"

"He admitted it to us," Frank said.

Captain Martinez's expression grew even more somber. He ran his hand slowly through his hair and said deliberately, "Boys, it's time we took a trip out to Rancho del Mar."

Two police cars escorted Frank and Joe in Rosa's Jeep on the way back to Señor Galvan's ranch. Captain Martinez drove the first one, and two officers followed in the other.

They drove past the scene where Ruperto had ambushed the van. They could see that the ambulance had already come and gone and that a lone guard sat in his police cruiser watching over the abandoned vehicle. Craning his neck to look back, Joe said, "When we first met him García seemed totally loyal to the *policía* and to Galvan. Captain Martinez must be pretty shocked about all this."

"That's right, Joe," Frank said. "He was by-the-book. But I realized he might not be one hundred percent clean when he showed up at Ray Don Stanley's warehouse the other night. He said he was working for Galvan then. Right now I'd be willing to bet he's operating on his own."

Within a half hour they pulled up to the hacienda. Rosa was there to meet them at the front door. "What happened?" she asked Frank. Before he could answer, she saw Captain Martinez and his two uniformed officers. She put her hand to her mouth, assuming the worst. "Rigo," she said. "Is he alive?"

"Rosa, we have no word about Rigo," Martinez said in a kind voice, "but we need to speak with your uncle. Is he here?"

"I'll get him," Rosa said. She led them into the living room and knocked softly on the study door.

"Uncle Ramon, Captain Martinez would like to see you," she said.

"Is it about Rigo?" Galvan asked, emerging from his study.

"We're not sure, Señor Galvan," Captain Martinez said. "But I must ask you some questions."

"As long as it's about Rigo," he said.

"Please be seated," the captain said.

"Captain, we don't have time for idle chat," Galvan said sternly. "We have one priority now, and that is finding my nephew."

Unflustered by the ranch owner's tone, Captain Martinez said, "Excuse me, Señor Galvan, I don't like this any better than you do, but we have reason to believe that you are involved in a weapons-smuggling operation."

A dead silence descended on the room. Galvan's mouth tightened, and he glanced quickly at Frank and Joe.

121

"Where did you hear this information?" Galvan finally said. "And what does it have to do with Rigo? How are you going to find my nephew if you start chasing gunrunning operations?"

"Do you deny the accusation?" Martinez said.

Again there was a long silence. Finally Galvan said in a weary voice, "No, *Capitán*. I do not deny it. I suppose these American boys told you about the shipment I was to receive this morning. Is that correct?"

"Yes," Captain Martinez said.

Galvan took a deep breath. He looked over at Rosa. "I'm afraid there's more," he said. "I've been trying to figure out a way to tell you all day, but I haven't been able to come up with the right words." He glanced over at Captain Martinez, who had taken his little notebook out of his pocket and was scribbling in it. "Now it doesn't look like I have much time left. And I want you to hear it from me."

"What is it, Uncle Ramon?" Rosa said. "What are you trying to tell us?"

"I know who kidnapped Rigo," Galvan said softly.

Chapter

13

"IT WAS RUPERTO GARCÍA," Galvan said.

"How did you find out?" Rosa said, shaking her head in disbelief. "How long have you known this? How long did you wait to tell us?"

In the moment of silence before Galvan answered, Rosa stood still, staring at her uncle. Then her eyes began to swim in tears. Galvan finally said, "I found out just yesterday. When Lieutenant García and I fought last night, I was trying to get more information out of him. He told me he was involved in the kidnapping but not where they were holding Rigo."

"Why didn't you tell us yesterday afternoon?" Rosa asked.

The anguish in Galvan's voice was unmistakable. "As I told you before, I had to hide my dealings with the Montañeros," he said. "But when García discovered that El Brujo was working for me, delivering arms to the rebels, he threatened to expose me to my business partners. He warned me not to tell anyone about his double-dealing. He said Rigo would be killed if I let on."

"What did he say, exactly?" Frank asked.

"He said he was in some kind of trouble with his partners and it was over the money. The partners are the ones actually holding Rigo. García is trying to set up another chance to collect the ransom. He said if I told anyone else about it, he would tell his partners that I had refused to pay, and they would kill Rigo instantly."

"Who are his partners?" Frank said.

"They are corrupt *policía*," Galvan said. "I don't know their names."

"I can find out who they are," Captain Martinez said. "García always had a few officers with whom he was particularly close." Galvan handed him the telephone.

While Captain Martinez was calling the station, Joe asked Señor Galvan, "Why would García want to blackmail you? Wasn't he well paid?"

"He must have wanted the big money fast. He told me he first thought of the plan when I hired him as a bodyguard. When he learned of Rigo's big bullfight," Galvan said, "he must have seen the opportunity to arrange for a public spectacle, a kidnapping that would generate as much publicity as possible, so the stakes would be high. Disguising the operation as a Montañero-run attack, he wouldn't be blamed. And with such a public act, I was sure to pay any amount to get Rigo back. He and his partners arranged to use disguised *policía* equipment—the helicopter, the truck, and all their weapons.

"When García discovered I was involved in supplying arms to the Montañeros, he went to see Ray Don Stanley without my knowledge, pretending to represent me."

"What did I tell you?" Frank said, looking at Joe. "When I saw him at the docks, he was just finding out for himself about the gunrunning operation."

Galvan continued, "Ruperto realized he could cut a double deal. We had the full amount for the kidnappers. He was the one who advised me not to put all of it in the satchel. He wanted to keep the rest for himself, cheating his partners out of their share. He said the money I gave him would keep him silent about the gunrunning operation. But I guess his partners started to suspect that he was lying to them."

"So García's little double-dealing went sour when they found out about the money," said Frank.

"That would explain why he was so confused

when the undercover cops on the bus got butchered," Joe said. "His partners found out he couldn't be trusted, and they killed his men."

Frank shook his head. "He realized he was just as responsible for the murder of those undercover cops."

Rosa had been quiet up until now. In a firm voice she said, "We must find Rigo. *Now*. Do you hear me?" Her voice was tinged with anger. She clenched and unclenched her jaw.

Frank said, "She's right. And we may not have much time. Now that García is acting on his own, he may do something even more desperate. Plus his partners have itchy trigger fingers, and they must be getting pretty nervous."

"They were expecting to be counting their ransom money by now," Joe said.

"Who knows where García lives?" Frank continued.

"I do," Rosa said. "It's right next to the bullfighting ring."

Captain Martinez had ended his telephone conversation and was listening carefully. "I can have his place crawling with *policía* in minutes," he said.

"Hold on a second," Joe said. "What if one of García's partners gets tipped off that we're on to his scam?"

"You're right," Captain Martinez said. "I should take care of this myself."

"We're going with you," Joe said.

"We will all go," Rosa said.

"Not Señor Galvan, I'm afraid," Captain Martinez said. "My men will have to take him down to the station in Matamoros."

"To jail?" Rosa said. She turned to look fearfully at her uncle.

"Do not worry about me, Rosa," Señor Galvan said. "I am prepared to face the consequences of my actions. If you can find Rigo alive and bring García and his partners to justice, then I will be able to live with my conscience."

Frank and Joe got into Rosa's Jeep. She was behind the wheel and they were following Captain Martinez's police cruiser down Rancho del Mar's long driveway. Joe saw a roadrunner racing alongside them, looking jaunty with its tail raised like a little flag.

"That could be García," Joe said, watching the long-limbed bird as it stayed just ahead of the Jeep. "He's fast and always seems to be one step ahead of us."

The roadrunner veered off into the brush as Rosa turned onto the highway. She gripped the wheel tighter, accelerating until she was tailgating Martinez's police cruiser. "Come on, step on it, Captain," she muttered.

"Careful, Rosa," Joe said. "We don't want

to go piling into the captain's car and get held up even longer."

"I seriously doubt it's a matter of minutes at this point," Frank said.

"What makes you so sure?" Rosa said. "You're the one who said we might not have much time."

They spent the rest of the drive to Matamoros in silence. Each of the three was wondering what lay ahead. Would a search of García's apartment shed light on his whereabouts? And if it did, would that help them catch up with him and track down Rigo's captors in time?

It was a Sunday, so traffic was light when they entered the city. García's neighborhood, which surrounded the bullfighting stadium, was full of rows of double-parked cars. There was a "spectacle" on, and it had drawn a large percentage of the city's population. They could hear the sound of the huge crowd shouting, "Olé!" as they arrived in front of García's apartment.

Martinez parked his cruiser in front of the building, while Rosa parked her Jeep across the street. As she and the Hardys climbed out of the Jeep, they saw Martinez gazing up at a second-story window. Frank followed the line of his gaze and saw a man's torso framed by the glass. Could it be García? he wondered. Before he could react, he heard gunshots—two of them. Martinez heard the shots, too, and he ran to the front doors of the building with his hand on his gun.

Joe started sprinting toward the building, with Rosa close behind. Frank yelled, "I'll cover the back," and he veered off to the driveway behind the apartment building.

Joe heard the crunch of a door being kicked in, and he sprinted up the stairs. He found Martinez kneeling over a body. The man was dressed in a police uniform. He'd been hit twice, once in the hand and once in the stomach.

Kneeling beside Captain Martinez, Joe said, "Do you know him?"

The captain nodded. "Sergeant Jorge Sanchez," he said. "He is one of Lieutenant García's closest friends on the force. "He—"

"Shh," Joe said. "He's trying to say something."

"Ruperto," the victim said weakly. "He wants the matador. But I wouldn't tell him."

"Where is Ruperto?" Captain Martinez said.

"Gone," Sanchez said, struggling for each breath. "He saw you coming."

Rosa appeared beside Joe and pushed past him. "Where is my brother, Rigo?" she said. "Where is my brother?" she repeated, grabbing the man by both shoulders and shaking him. "You can't let García get away with this. You have to tell us."

"He's—he's—" Sanchez swallowed hard and said, "He's going to meet *el momento de la verdad,*" then he slipped into unconsciousness.

"What did he say?" Joe asked.

"He said he's going to meet his moment of truth," Rosa said.

Chapter

14

"WHERE DID THEY TAKE HIM?" Rosa asked the man, shaking him again in the hope he could say a few more words. But it was too late.

Captain Martinez went to the phone and made an emergency call for an ambulance. He was careful to pull his handkerchief out of his pocket and use it to pick up the receiver so as not to smudge any fingerprints that might be on it already.

Joe bent over Sergeant Sanchez and began carefully searching his pockets. Aside from the usual loose change, keys, and wallet, he found a photo. He picked it up gingerly by its edges and showed it to Rosa.

It showed Rigo, staring straight into the camera, his lip cut and swollen, his left eye almost closed shut. He stood against a white-washed adobe wall. The photograph itself was torn along all four edges into the shape of a coffin.

"They were probably going to use this when they contacted Señor Galvan to collect the ransom again," Joe said, "but García beat them to the punch."

"Let me see that photo," Captain Martinez said, using his handkerchief again. "It could provide some clues as to where Rigo is being held. Rosa, do you recognize this wall?"

She bent over the photo, trying to jog her memory, but she couldn't remember ever having seen it.

Meanwhile Frank had rounded the corner at the back of the apartment building, running at full tilt. He saw that the parking lot was surrounded by a high fence, providing few avenues of escape. He slowed down and scanned the rows of neatly parked cars. Then he checked the back of the building, looking in the doorway and behind the garbage Dumpsters. After the crack of those two gunshots, the building had fallen silent. In the background he could hear the cries of "Olé! Olé!" as the stadium erupted in another celebration.

Frank began to develop the uncanny sensation of being watched. He glanced up at a second-story window, where a frightened neighbor was leaning out and peering at him.

"Did you see anyone?" Frank shouted up at the middle-aged woman.

"*Qué?*" she replied. "*No hablo inglés.*"

Frank couldn't come up with the right phrase in Spanish. Finally he held up his hand, finger extended like the barrel of a gun, and said, "Did you see *pow! Pow!*"

"*Sí,*" said the woman. She cupped her hand behind her ear. "*Yo lo he oido.*"

"No, did you *see* anyone?" Frank called up to the woman in the window, pointing to his eye.

The woman shook her head. "*No, no lo he visto.*"

She hadn't seen anyone come into the parking lot. Frank waved and said, "*Gracias,*" then started to walk back around to the front of the building.

As he came out of the parking lot, he heard the screech of tires peeling away on the street. He raced back around to the front of the building. He saw two tread marks on the pavement and smoke from the burning rubber. Beyond that, already a block ahead, was a white sedan. It took the corner up ahead at high speed, leaning heavily and fishtailing out of sight.

"Joe," Frank shouted up to the apartment window from where they had heard the gunshots. Joe's face appeared; he quickly slid up the window and leaned out. "The shooter is heading south in a white, four-door sedan,"

Frank said. "I didn't get the license plate number."

"Okay," Joe said. "Captain Martinez will call it in."

"Have Rosa throw down the keys to the Jeep," Frank said. "I'll go after him and see if I can pick up a trail."

Joe poked his head back in the apartment and then back out. "Negative, Frank" was Joe's reply. "He's already out of the neighborhood by now, and the chief says they'll catch him inside the city limits. Besides, there's something up here I think you should see."

Frank peered in the direction the shooter had gone. I hope the police are willing to grab him, he thought. Even if he is one of their own.

Upstairs, Frank found Rosa and Joe staring at a photograph. Looking over their shoulders, Frank saw it was a picture of Rigo, most likely taken in the last two days by the kidnappers.

"I found it in the victim's shirt pocket," Joe said, indicating the sergeant, who was flat out on the floor in a small but growing pool of blood. The captain pressed a towel to his wounds.

"Is he going to be all right?" Frank asked, nodding at the unconscious man. They could hear the wail of sirens in the distance.

"I called an ambulance," Captain Martinez said. Then he went over to the phone again and started giving orders in high-speed Spanish. Frank guessed he was calling for units to pursue the white sedan and to back them up.

"García must have attacked him because he wouldn't tell him where they're holding Rigo," Joe said.

"Maybe he told him, and Ruperto shot him anyway," Rosa said.

"The way the lieutenant has been acting since yesterday, I wouldn't be surprised," Joe said.

"I have a feeling he spotted us from the window," Frank said. "I guess we interrupted his little interrogation." He asked Rosa, "What does *el momento de la verdad* mean?"

"It is the moment of truth during the bullfight when either the bull—or the matador—is killed," she answered.

"What exactly do you think he meant by that?" Frank said.

"Just what you said before," Joe said. "That we don't have much time. That they're threatening to kill Rigo if we don't come up with the money right away."

"What's our next move?" Frank asked. He glanced first at Rosa, then at Joe. "Any ideas?"

"My guess is García will try to contact Señor Galvan," Joe said. "Or maybe he'll try to find one of his other partners and pump him for information on where they're holding Rigo."

"I didn't see the driver of the white car,"

Frank said. "So we're not even sure that it was García. It could have been one of the other kidnappers. Rigo could have been in the car."

"Don't worry about that," Captain Martinez said, hanging up the telephone. "I just put out an all-points bulletin on García and on that white sedan. Whoever is in it, we've definitely got him in a box. It's just a matter of time before we flush him out into the open."

"What should we do?" Rosa said, clutching the photograph to her chest. "This box you speak of is working against Rigo. He is still the prisoner of the corrupt *policía*. With my uncle under arrest, the prospects for a large ransom have disappeared."

"She's right," Frank said. "They have no use for Rigo anymore, dead or alive."

"I'm going to have to file a full report on this," Captain Martinez said, nodding toward the unconscious sergeant on the floor. "The safest place for you kids is back at the *rancho*. I will arrange for a police escort immediately."

"No," said Rosa. "We're not going back. There's no time."

Frank was looking at the photograph she clutched to her chest. Obviously nobody had told her not to touch anything at a crime scene. Her fingerprints were probably all over it now.

Then Frank remembered something odd about the photo, something he'd noticed the first time he looked at it. "Let me see that," he said, gently pulling the photograph from Rosa's hands.

Rigo's face, bruised though it was, held a defiant look, with his eyes glaring straight into the camera. His matador's uniform was tattered and a sleeve was torn. The adobe wall behind him revealed no clues about where the picture had been taken.

It was Rigo's hands that drew Frank's attention. He looked at them closely. One of them was balled up in an unusual way, making a fist, but with the index finger and the pinky each sticking straight out. At first Frank thought the fingers might have been broken so that Rigo couldn't bend them to make a fist.

Joe interrupted Frank's concentration. "What are you looking at?" he asked.

"It's his hand, see?" Frank replied, pointing at the image. "It's sort of balled up, but it looks like—"

"He's making a bull's horns," Joe finished. "Like two horns, with his knuckles as the head between them."

Rosa and the Hardys puzzled over Rigo's secret hand signal for a few more moments.

"Look at that clever boy," Rosa said finally. "He's sending a message in English so the kidnappers couldn't pick it up. One of his fingers is pointing to the ring on his other hand," she said.

"His hand is a bull and he's pointing to his ring," Joe said.

"The bullring," Frank said. "He's telling us where he is."

Rosa snapped her fingers. "The bullfight," she said. "That's what Sanchez meant when he said the moment of truth."

"Let's go," Joe said. "We've got to get over to the stadium and search the place. They've probably got Rigo hidden underneath it somewhere."

"Hold on just a minute," Captain Martinez said. "You can't just leave the scene of a crime like this. You're all important witnesses, and I'm going to need statements from each of you."

"We'll have plenty of time for that later, Captain," said Frank, grabbing Rosa's hand and heading for the door. "Can you call for some backup units at the stadium? I have a feeling we're going to need them."

As the three teenagers raced out the door, Captain Martinez shook his head and yelled after them, "Don't do anything until the reinforcements arrive. They'll be there in a few minutes."

"Yes, sir," Joe shouted over his shoulder, following Rosa and Frank down the stairs.

As they ran the two blocks to the stadium, Frank managed to congratulate Rosa on her detective work. "You really have a knack for putting two and two together," he said. "Who would have guessed that Rigo would send a message in English?"

"He's my brother," she said. "I suppose we think alike."

"How are we going to get into the stadium?" Joe asked. "We don't have tickets."

"They know me at the ticket window," Rosa said. "I can talk us in."

"Not safe," Frank said. "If one of the kidnappers spots you, then we blow our chance to surprise them. Is there any other way in?"

"Yes," Rosa said. "The bull pens." She veered off toward the rear of the stadium. "El Brujo used to bring me and Rigo here when we were children. We used to watch him talk to the bulls before they went into the ring."

"He talked to them?" Frank asked.

"Yes," Rosa replied. "He said it gave them courage to face their own moments of truth."

The stockyards were deserted, and the threesome slipped into one of the pens easily. Hoof marks and droppings in the dust suggested that the bull in the corral had recently entered the ring. Above their heads, they could hear the crowd roaring. There was plenty of action in the ring.

"In here," Rosa said, ducking into a wooden chute. "This leads into the ring."

"We can't go into the ring," Frank said.

"Of course not," Rosa said. "But we can watch from the chute."

The chute ended abruptly in a movable wooden wall, gouged and splintered by many a raging bull's horns. Joe saw a pulley that would raise the gate when the time came for the bull to enter the ring.

Gaps in the planks provided a narrow view of the ring. With their eyes pressed up against the rough wood, they didn't see any movement. The ring seemed empty. Then Joe saw the flash of a red cape, closer than he expected. A matador moved into view, with his back to them.

Suddenly the matador yanked the red cape away, twirling in a flash of color. From behind the cape loomed the massive black shape of the bull, galloping at full speed directly at them.

Joe hardly had time to react. He stepped back a split second before the bull slammed hard into the wooden gate. The gate shuddered violently with the impact, and Joe stumbled. At the same instant, Joe heard the angry snort of the bull as it turned back toward the matador in the ring.

Joe tripped on something as he stumbled backward. He lost his balance and fell, expecting to land on the seat of his pants in the dirt. But he didn't land in a heap. Someone caught him. Someone who had sneaked up behind him as he fell.

"Didn't I tell you, *hijo?*" said a familiar voice in a thick Spanish accent. "Always keep your eye on the bull."

Chapter

15

JOE TURNED AND LOOKED at the person who had caught him. It was the old matador with that familiar quizzical half smile, half frown on his weathered face.

"El Brujo," he said. "What are you doing here?"

Rosa and Frank whirled around, too, and Rosa rushed over to embrace him.

Smiling, obviously rather pleased with himself, El Brujo said, "Careful, *niña*. I am a bruised old man, and I might break."

His eye was still swollen from the beating he'd received, but Joe could see no evidence of pain in his face.

"Where's Zeta?" Frank asked. "Isn't it dangerous to be here? We thought you were going to disappear. You're a fugitive from the law."

"Zeta has gone back to Rancho Sonora," El Brujo replied. "And me? What could the law want to do with me anymore? They found out I am only a caretaker of bulls—nothing more, nothing less. I thought I'd come see another bullfight. A man my age has few pleasures, and watching a good match between matador and bull is one of them."

"Rigo is here," Rosa said, explaining the hand signals in the photograph of Rigo.

El Brujo chuckled. "He is a clever one, my little Rigo. He has learned his lessons well."

"We don't know exactly where they're holding him," Joe said. "We do know that one of his kidnappers told us Rigo was going to face his *momento de la verdad.*"

"Let me see that photograph," El Brujo said. He studied it for a moment, then said, "There's only one place in this stadium where they have adobe walls. Follow me, little ones." He climbed over the chute wall and led them to a staircase that went down to a feed storage room in the basement.

At the bottom of the stairs, El Brujo paused to listen. Pointing down a hallway that led away from the room under the stadium seats, he pressed his finger to his lips. "Down there," he whispered. "One guard at the door."

Rosa whispered, "There are four of us, and just one of them. Let's take him."

142

"There are probably others," Frank cautioned her. "And they're all definitely armed."

"I could circle around," Joe said. "Maybe there's a way to get at them from the other side."

"Let's skip the circling-around part," Frank said. He found a wooden plank about the size of a baseball bat on the straw-covered floor. He thunked it twice on the floor.

Instantly Joe flattened himself against the one wall inside the doorway. Frank took the other side, motioning for Rosa and El Brujo to stay where they were.

Standing in plain sight, Rosa and El Brujo kept their faces impassive while the sound of the guard's footsteps approached.

Joe saw the guard poke the muzzle of a rifle into the room, pointing it at Rosa and El Brujo. He aimed a swift kick upward, hitting the gun solidly. The guard fired, but the bullet whizzed over Rosa's head. Frank swung the board hard, connecting with the guard's throat and sending him down, gagging. Joe leaped on him, knocking the rifle aside, and delivered a powerful punch to his jaw that knocked the man out.

Rosa leaped over the guard's prone body, ran a short way down the hallway, and pounded on the door where the guard had stood. "Rigo!" she shouted. "It's me, Rosa!"

"Rosa?" came the muffled cry from within. *"Es tú?"*

"Sí," she said. Looking down the hallway at Joe, she said, "The key. Get it from the guard."

Joe searched the unconscious man's body, but he could find nothing. "Somebody else must have them," he said.

"Then we'll break it down," Rosa said.

The next sound Joe heard was not Rosa trying to kick down the door, but the unmistakable click of a revolver's trigger being cocked.

Joe glanced up and saw Ruperto García, one arm wrapped around Rosa's neck. His other hand held a revolver to her head.

"I've been looking forward to this meeting," García said. "I thought you would catch up to me eventually."

At the sound of García's voice, Frank crowded into the narrow hallway along with Joe and El Brujo. "How did you find us?" Frank demanded.

"I followed you," replied Ruperto. "After I left my apartment, when you stumbled on my interrogation of my former partner, I doubled back on foot. The other guy escaped in his car. I saw you come running out of the building and head over here to the bullring. As it turns out, you led me straight to Rigo."

"Let her go, García," Frank said. "It's not worth it." He started to move slowly toward the lieutenant, holding out his hands to show he wasn't armed. He kept moving cautiously forward, talking the whole time. "Captain Martinez knows about you. Everybody knows. No matter what you do to us, they'll still catch you."

"I do not deny it," García said. "My plan appears to have backfired. When I heard they took Galvan into custody, I knew I would never see any of the money."

Behind Frank, El Brujo was also advancing on García. As they moved forward, the lieutenant inched back, taking Rosa with him.

"Stay back," García warned. "Or I'll blow her brains out." Behind him was another gate, this one smaller than the one used for the bull, and not so heavily reinforced.

"You wouldn't do that to Rosa," Frank said. He had to keep talking, keep García occupied and hope that he would let down his guard for just one second. "I thought you cared about her."

A slight grin cracked García's grim face. "Of course I care about her, but that will not stop me from killing her," he said. "To tell you the truth, I like you and your brother, but that won't stop me from taking you down, too. If I'm going to go, I'm going to take as many as I can with me."

With that, he shoved Rosa hard toward Frank, which gave him just enough time to lean his shoulder against the door behind him and push out.

Frank caught Rosa, but he was blinded momentarily by the bright shaft of light that flooded through the open door as García shoved his way outside into the bullfighting ring. There was also a big inrush of sound as the roar of the crowd swept over them.

Joe ducked out the door and started after García. He'd only run a few strides when, dazzled by the sunlight, he slowed to a trot. Above him, he saw the stadium full of spectators rising on all sides. Thousands of people filled the stands like so many multicolored dots lining the stadium, some of them waving banners, most of them cheering. It was an overwhelming sight after the small, dank spaces underneath the stadium.

The crowd rose to its feet and there was a collective gasp when García ran into the ring, followed by Joe. Joe saw García ahead of him and to his left, still running.

Apparently the lieutenant did not see the bull in the center of the ring. But the bull saw him. Suddenly ignoring the matador, the massive beast followed the darting form of García. It swung its powerful head and neck, and then it took a few steps in García's direction.

The crowd grew ominously silent. Every eye in the stadium strained to see what would happen between the running gunman and the powerful bull. Perhaps it was this sudden hush, as every breath in the stadium seemed to draw inward, that caused García to slow to a trot. He stopped and looked up around him. He must have only just realized he was trapped in the ring with a menacing bull and at least one human pursuer.

In the brief, eerie hush, Joe heard El Brujo's voice coming from behind him. "Keep your eye on the bull, *hijo.*"

That's when Joe saw the big animal start to move. First a few tentative steps, then a trot as the bull lowered its horns and, gathering speed, aimed itself at García.

Joe heard voices in the crowd start to shout, "El Brujo! El Brujo!" Joe realized that the old magician had scurried past him and was heading toward the stunned matador across the ring.

Meanwhile, seeing that the bull had fixed him in its sights, García turned and broke into a dead run. He was heading for the side of the ring. Joe could see he wasn't going to make it. The bull was already in full gallop and quickly closed the distance between them.

At the last possible second, García dodged to the right, skidding and tumbling into the sand, escaping the bull's horns by inches. The furious beast thundered past him, raking its horns through the space where García had just been.

The giant animal turned, snorting with rage and foaming at the mouth. It dug its hooves into the dirt and charged again before García had a chance to stand up.

Moving faster than Joe thought possible, El Brujo stepped between the bull and García. He swung the red cape in front of the bull's face, temporarily distracting it. As the cape passed over the bull's eyes, it spun around, wildly attempting to drive its horns into the maddening sea of red. The crowd went wild, letting out a great shout of triumph as their beloved El Brujo executed a perfect *verónica* in front of their eyes for the first time in years.

García finally dragged himself to his feet, but he was unsteady.

When he caught sight of El Brujo, standing not ten feet away, García fixed a glassy stare on the old matador. Joe couldn't figure out who was more enraged, the lieutenant or the bull.

Unable to reach either of them in time, Joe watched in horror as the desperate lieutenant aimed his pistol at El Brujo and fired. "No," Joe shouted instinctively, and started running toward García.

But the bull got to García first. Coming at him from the side, the massive head of the enraged beast lifted him up high and tossed him more than twenty feet up as if he were a rag doll. The gun flew from his hands, and he landed hard in the dust. The bull did not stop there. Again he scooped up the struggling García and tossed him high with a vicious, twisting jab of the horns.

Joe heard García scream as a horn pierced his side. Twice more the bull gored García, until his battered body fell to the dirt, lifeless.

Meanwhile, with the bull occupied, Joe raced to El Brujo's side. His eyes were wide open and he lay on his side, grimacing. Kneeling beside El Brujo in the red dirt, Joe was relieved to see that the bullet had passed through his shoulder. "Are you all right?" he asked the wounded bullfighter.

"Yes," he replied weakly, "but there is no time to lose. Take the *muleta*. It's your only chance to get out of here alive."

"No way," Joe said. "I'm not ready."

"Then you must get ready," the old man said fiercely. "The bull has tasted blood, and he will be hungry for more."

Joe looked up and realized El Brujo was right. The bull stood over his motionless prey, bellowing and snorting. It swung its head around, fixed its eyes on Joe, and took a few steps in his direction.

"Take the *muleta*," El Brujo urged.

Joe took the cape from El Brujo, but as soon as he did, he regretted it. The bull caught sight of the red cloth and started to gallop toward it. Joe backed away from El Brujo's prone body. He felt as if the muscles in his legs were turning to jelly. He tried to brace himself but stumbled and almost fell.

The raging bull charged at Joe, lowering its head. Joe fought the urge to shut his eyes and wait for the impact. He held the shimmering cape in front of him and forced himself to focus on the onrushing horns. At the last possible moment he stepped aside and the locomotive-size beast galloped past within a hairsbreadth, its horns searching for Joe's flesh beneath the cape but finding only air.

The bull turned without a pause and rushed at Joe again. Again he deftly sidestepped the bull, dodging the horns. He became aware of the crowd shouting, "Olé! Olé! Bravo!" each time the bull attempted to batter him.

Out of the corner of his eye, Joe saw the young matador waving frantically from behind the wooden barrier on the other side of the ring. With the bull momentarily pausing after his last charge, his sides heaving and his black hide glistening with sweat, Joe managed to sidle up to the barrier. He handed the cape to the young man and ducked behind the thick wooden barrier.

With help from his team of assistants, the matador managed to herd the bull out of the ring and back down the chute.

On that day, Joe realized as he caught his

breath, the "moment of truth" had not been for the bull but for Lieutenant Ruperto García.

With the bull safely out of the ring, Frank and Rosa rushed over to where El Brujo lay crumpled on the red sand. "I'm all right," the old matador managed to say, gritting his teeth against the pain. "They just need to sew up this hole in my shoulder."

As the stretcher bearers carted him out of the ring, El Brujo managed a weak wave with his good arm. The crowd, on its feet, went wild.

Hundreds of fans dropped into the ring from the seats above, celebrating the splendid performance. Frank tracked down his brother in the jubilant crowd.

"Congratulations," Frank said, shaking Joe's hand and clapping him on the back. "It looks like you passed your first real test as a matador."

Joe laughed. "Thanks," he said. "But I don't think I'll make a profession out of it."

Joe happened to glance up at the crowd in the stands. He spotted a familiar figure bent over the ringside fence, waving. It was their father, Fenton. Joe grabbed Frank's arm and they went over to the wall.

"What are you doing here, Dad?" Joe yelled over the noise of the crowd.

"I'm the one who should be asking that question," Fenton shouted back. "I came to see a bullfight. Too bad I didn't know it was going to be my son's debut as a matador. I would have paid for a better seat."

"He was pretty good, don't you think, Dad?" Frank said. "And the best thing is—"

Frank was about to tell their dad they had found Rigo safe and sound when the crowd let out a giant roar and all three Hardys looked to see what the commotion was.

Over by the matador's entrance to the ring, a squad of police, led by Captain Martinez, had emerged with a dazed and weakened Rigo Galvan, still in his suit of lights. He gazed up at the crowd and squinted against the sun, then raised his hand in a salute. The crowd urged him into the center of the ring. Shouts of "El Puma! El Puma!" rained down from the stands. Rosa ran to his side and embraced him.

Then another chant started to build. "El Niño! El Niño!" the crowd began to shout.

"What does that mean?" Joe said.

"It means 'The Boy,' " Frank said, laughing. "They're talking about you, Joe. You're the boy today!"

Joe pretended to be offended. "I hate it when people call me that," he said. But he was smiling, and at Frank's prodding, he walked to the center of the ring.

The crowd cheered loudly as Joe Hardy, novice bullfighter from Bayport, U.S.A., stood beside Rigo and Rosa and took a deep bow.

152

Frank and Joe's next case:

Joe Hardy has a new interest in chemistry, and her name is Yvonne Ziebarth. Having quit her graduate studies at the university, she's just signed on at Bayport High to teach, and she's made up of all the right elements to get a reaction out of Joe: She's young, she's cute . . . and she's the number one suspect in a murder. Her former supervisor was killed by a deadly chemical, and all the evidence points to one conclusion: Yvonne Ziebarth deliberately mislabeled the poison in order to set up her professor. Convinced that *she's* the one being set up, the Hardys are doing some research of their own . . . and if they're not careful, the findings could prove fatal . . . in *Bad Chemistry*, Case #110 in The Hardy Boys Casefiles™.

Now your younger brothers or sisters
can take a walk down Fear Street....

R·L·STINE'S

GHOSTS OF FEAR STREET

1 Hide and Shriek
52941-2 / $3.50
2 Who's Been Sleeping in My Grave?
52942-0 / $3.50
3 Attack of the Aqua Apes
52943-9 / $3.99
4 Nightmare in 3-D
52944-7 / $3.99
5 Stay Away From the Treehouse
52945-5 / $3.99
6 Eye of the Fortuneteller
52946-3 / $3.99

A scary new series for the
younger reader from **R.L. Stine**